"I hope your appreciates you."

Kate fixed him with a coquettish smile. "How lucky she is having a man with so many talents. It isn't every day one comes across a man who can pitch a tent in the dark and kill snakes before breakfast and then, on top of all that, cook a wonderful meal!"

"Indeed, I have many rare talents," Vittorio agreed with a smile. "But don't waste your compliments on me, *señorita.* Sweet as they are, they will not change my mind. Just as soon as we have finished breakfast, we'll be setting out for Bagu Bayo where I shall deposit you with my friends who will take you back to Manila."

Kate could have kicked him! She might have known he would be immune to flattery!

Stephanie Howard is a British author whose two ambitions since childhood were to see the world and to write. Her first venture into the world was a four-year stay in Italy, learning the language and supporting herself by writing short stories. Then her sensible side brought her back to London to read Social Administrations at the London School of Economics. She has held various editorial posts at magazines such as *Reader's Digest, Vanity Fair,* and *Women's Own,* as well as writing free-lance for *Cosmopolitan, Good Housekeeping* and *The Observer.* She recently spent six years happily trotting around the globe, although she has now returned to the U.K. to write romance novels.

Books by Stephanie Howard

HARLEQUIN ROMANCE

3093—MASTER OF GLEN CRANNACH
3112—AN IMPOSSIBLE PASSION
3153—WICKED DECEIVER

HARLEQUIN PRESENTS

1098—RELUCTANT PRISONER
1130—DARK LUCIFER
1168—HIGHLAND TURMOIL
1273—BRIDE FOR A PRICE
1307—KISS OF THE FALCON
1450—A BRIDE FOR STRATHALLANE

Don't miss any of our special offers. Write to us at the following address for information on our newest releases.

Harlequin Reader Service
P.O. Box 1397, Buffalo, NY 14240
Canadian address: P.O. Box 603,
Fort Erie, Ont. L2A 5X3

ROMANTIC JOURNEY
Stephanie Howard

Harlequin Books

TORONTO • NEW YORK • LONDON
AMSTERDAM • PARIS • SYDNEY • HAMBURG
STOCKHOLM • ATHENS • TOKYO • MILAN
MADRID • WARSAW • BUDAPEST • AUCKLAND

If you purchased this book without a cover you should be aware
that this book is stolen property. It was reported as "unsold and
destroyed" to the publisher, and neither the author nor the
publisher has received any payment for this "stripped book."

Original hardcover edition published in 1991
by Mills & Boon Limited

ISBN 0-373-03195-5

Harlequin Romance first edition May 1992

ROMANTIC JOURNEY

Copyright © 1991 by Stephanie Howard.
All rights reserved. Except for use in any review, the reproduction or utilization
of this work in whole or in part in any form by any electronic, mechanical or
other means, now known or hereafter invented, including xerography,
photocopying and recording, or in any information storage or retrieval system,
is forbidden without the permission of the publisher, Harlequin Enterprises
Limited, 225 Duncan Mill Road, Don Mills, Ontario, Canada M3B 3K9.

All the characters in this book have no existence outside the imagination of
the author and have no relation whatsoever to anyone bearing the same name
or names. They are not even distantly inspired by any individual known or
unknown to the author, and all incidents are pure invention.

® are Trademarks registered in the United States Patent and Trademark Office
and in other countries.

Printed in U.S.A.

CHAPTER ONE

A BEAD of sweat trickled down the back of Kate's leg and landed with a plop on the heel of her sandal. Instantly, another one followed.

With a sigh, she leaned back in the rear seat of the taxi and mopped her brow with a clump of tissues. The heat, here in Manila, was even worse than it had been in Hong Kong—and, at least, in Hong Kong, all the taxis had been properly air-conditioned. This Manila cab was like a furnace, and winding down the window had only made matters worse. The blast of steamy hot air in her face had very nearly suffocated her on the spot. Better to expire slowly, by degrees, she had decided, hurriedly winding the window back up.

Besides, it was marginally less noisy with the windows closed—though only very marginally, she conceded, as an overloaded jeepney came careering alongside them, horn blaring, chickens squawking, threatening to run them off the road.

It was their third close encounter with a jeepney in almost as many minutes, and little wonder, Kate had to admit. These colourful little buses, with their elaborately painted bodywork—all flowers and birds and exotic looking animals—swarmed in their hundreds along teeming Roxas Boulevard, the central artery of the Philippines' capital city, looking for all the world as though they'd escaped

from a fun-fair, and creating merry havoc as they
went on their way.

Yet, in spite of their faintly homicidal tend-
encies, they all had cute, slightly saucy names. Sexy
Suzy was the name of this latest one. With a weak
smile Kate shook her head and sighed. How could
anyone think of such things in this heat?

'Here, miss! We arrived!'

The cab driver was yelling at her over his
shoulder, as, with a sudden kamikaze manoeuvre
that left Sexy Suzy behind in a cloud of dust, he
swung straight through the lines of traffic and skit-
tered to a halt at the side of the road. With a gap-
toothed smile, he jabbed a finger streetwards at the
crumbling façade of the building that flanked them.

'Ramos Worldwide!' he announced with satisfaction, echoing the immodest legend painted above
the door.

Kate followed his jabbing finger with her eyes
and inwardly sighed a sigh of relief. So Ramos
Worldwide, unimpressive as it looked, really did
exist, after all. Ever since she had left Hong Kong,
with only a scribbled name and address to go on,
she had feared she might be off on some wild-goose
chase. The word of a brief acquaintance in a Hong
Kong bar was not, after all, the most reliable of
leads!

But Ramos Worldwide *did* exist—and now her
next task was to try to discover if the lost tribe of
Cabayan existed, too. That was the hope that had
brought her here. And her answer lay behind those
peeling, sun-baked walls.

'Here.' She fumbled in her bag for pesos as the driver named his fare, quickly calculating the tip before handing him a pile of notes.

The tip was evidently sufficient. 'Ramos Worldwide, fourth floor,' he told her with another cheerful, gap-toothed grin. Then he stretched behind him to open the rear door for her. 'Have a nice day, miss!' he added.

'I hope so,' Kate murmured. And a successful one, too, she added silently as she climbed from the cab and stepped into the steam-bath heat of Manila. A great deal depended on the outcome of this venture. Her future and, more importantly, the future of her brother. It was for Liam's sake that she had come.

As the cab departed, Kate paused for a moment and looked around her to get her bearings. This was her very first visit to the Philippines and she was still feeling slightly overawed by it all. It was so totally, so vibrantly different from any other country she had ever visited, and light years away from her last stop, Hong Kong. Exotically, chaotically, Eastern, yet with a superficial sprinkling of American pizzazz. That 'Have a nice day!' from the toothless cab driver, who probably had no more than a dozen words of English, somehow neatly summed the place up.

She shook back her head of red-gold hair, that clung damply to the back of her neck, and briskly smoothed her heat-crumpled skirt. Somehow, she had a feeling that before her lay far more than just the scoop of her journalistic career—a once-in-a-lifetime adventure as well and possibly, just possibly, the solution to all her problems.

With a spring in her step she marched across the pavement, a slim, vital figure in a stylish peach two-piece, shoulders back, ready for action, a gleam of determination in her emerald Irish eyes.

Fourth floor, the cabby had told her, and the list of occupants she found in the hallway bore that piece of intelligence out. So far so good, she decided optimistically, stepping into the rickety old lift. And suddenly she was feeling half human again. The building was air-conditioned and deliciously cool.

After a brief ride the elevator stopped with a shudder, then with a creak and a groan the doors slowly opened—to reveal a surprisingly sumptuous office, carpeted wall to wall in a soft, verdant green. Instantly, Kate's spirits shot up another notch. In spite of its somewhat seedy exterior, Ramos Worldwide had every appearance of a set-up to be reckoned with!

An exceedingly pretty Filipina sat perched behind the reception desk. She beamed a welcome at her flushed, rumpled visitor. 'Good afternoon. What can I do for you, please?'

Kate approached the desk, her confidence growing. This organisation was evidently efficient, too. 'I'm Kate O'Shaughnessy,' she explained, 'a reporter with *Deadline* magazine in London. I don't have an appointment, I'm afraid—I was unable to track down your phone number and I just arrived in Manila this morning—but I've come to see Mr Ramos, if that's possible. I'd like to talk to him about the Cabayan expedition.'

The girl met her request with a smile of apology. 'Mr Ramos is in a meeting right now.' She nodded discreetly towards her boss's office door. 'But if you'd care to take a seat in the meantime...' she waved a glossy pink fingernail in the direction of a leather sofa '...I'll speak to him as soon as he's free.'

'Thanks.' Kate nodded gratefully, thoroughly impressed. As well as efficient, this company was co-operative. Everything she could have hoped for. On buoyant strides, she headed for the leather sofa—but halfway across the floor was as far as she got.

Suddenly, Ramos's office door burst open, seeming almost to explode right off its hinges, and a tall, striking man with midnight black hair came striding through it, like a human whirlwind, straight into Kate's path.

He missed colliding with her by a centimetre, drew himself up, then paused to scowl down at her, an anger like hellfire burning from his face. 'Get out of my way!'

His eyes burned right through her, eyes like coals, set in a face that, even in repose, would have sent a tremor through any mortal soul. For it was a face of vibrant, startling power—with spare high cheekbones, straight nose and strong jawline, and a wide mobile mouth, suited to wild extremes of passion. It was a face at once both savage and noble, the face of a man, one sensed instinctively, with whom it would not be wise to trifle.

And, right now, that face absolutely burned with fury. Rage leapt from every dark line and shadow. And every sinew of his powerfully muscular body seemed to vibrate with the potency of his wrath.

Like an unleashed whirlwind he stood before Kate, poised to demolish every obstacle in his path.

Kate had frozen to the spot, her normally quick-thinking responses momentarily deserting her. But, before he could proceed to demolish her, a voice behind him spoke—the voice of a man whom Kate hadn't even noticed, but who had followed the dark whirlwind through the door.

'You don't scare me, Esquerez!' he piped, his entire demeanour belying his brave words. 'Don't think you can come here and start throwing your weight about—any more than you can in Cabayan! You keep your nose out of Ramos business, or, I promise you, you'll end up sorry!'

As the whirlwind spun round to face his accuser, like a tiger pouncing on a gnat, a bell suddenly went off inside Kate's head. Could she possibly have heard correctly? Had Ramos called the man 'Esquerez'?

She frowned at his back as he took a step towards Ramos and demanded in a deep growl of a voice, 'Are you trying to threaten me, by any chance? I wouldn't advise that! I don't take kindly to threats!' Could this possibly be the same Esquerez, she was wondering, with whose company she herself had crossed swords in Hong Kong?

Whoever he was he was a rampant bully, she decided with a wave of sympathy for Ramos. For at least on a purely physical level the slender Filipino was clearly out of his class.

The dark whirlwind, who stood now with his back to Kate, his jet-black hair curling thickly over his collar, towered a good half-metre over his hapless adversary, like a mountain scowling down at a molehill. The powerful shoulders and strongly-muscled arms that strained beneath the faded cotton T-shirt could have catapulted Ramos through the window with the ease of a baseball player fielding a ball. The long, lean legs beneath the faded blue jeans reached almost to the other man's chest and spoke of a whiplash speed of reflex that would leave most men, and certainly Ramos, standing.

And yet, Ramos, to his credit, was fighting back, like a game Yorkshire terrier confronted by a bull. 'Get out of my office, Esquerez!' he commanded in his nervous, high-pitched voice. 'And stay out of it—and out of my business—for good!'

So she had heard right! The man's name *was* Esquerez. No doubt *the* Esquerez, judging by the scene before her. And instantly Kate's sympathy for Ramos quadrupled. She regarded the dark whirlwind through disapproving eyes, as he snarled at Ramos with a voice like scorching cinders, 'Don't worry, I'm leaving. I've delivered the message I came to give you. But don't think I'll be staying out of your business! Take my word for it, you'll be hearing more from me!'

With that final message, the whirlwind turned on his heel—and very nearly went crashing once more straight into Kate.

He frowned down at her with those burning dark eyes, so close now she could see they were ebony-black. And their blackness and their intensity seemed to pierce right through her, driving like lances into the back of her head.

With those eyes on her face, he demanded harshly, 'I thought I told you to get out of my way? Are you deliberately trying to irritate me?'

Black eyes and emerald met and collided. Then the emerald eyes narrowed. 'Irritate you? I wouldn't dream of it! But, all the same, I should point out that it's you who happens to be in *my* way!' And she felt a rush of defiant pleasure sweep through her as one raven-black eyebrow arched upwards in surprise. He had clearly anticipated a more docile response.

Kate half expected him to push her aside. After all, he had the rough manners for it! But, instead, she saw the wide mouth quirk at the corners and a flash of amusement momentarily soften the dark eyes.

'So, *señorita*, you are in the mood for a debate?' The laser-like gaze travelled over her face, absorbing every detail, she sensed, in an instant. Then his expression became hard again. 'Alas, however, I am not, so I would be obliged if you would just move out of my way.'

Close to, that wide and passionate mouth was remarkably well-defined, Kate found herself observing: the lower lip narrow and curved tautly, like a crossbow, the lower one generous and full of sensuous promise. As he spoke, she caught a glimpse of remarkably white teeth, their whiteness made even more startlingly vivid by the contrasting mahogany tan of his skin.

And she smiled an illogical inward smile as she detected that the aggressive, thrusting chin was host to a perfectly disarming indentation. Kate had always had a weakness for cleft chins.

But this was no time for weakness. His impatience plainly growing, he was demanding, 'Well, do you plan to move, or do I have to move you?'

Kate drew herself up. 'Why should I move? As I told you already, it's you who're in *my* way!'

She was pushing her luck. She could sense that quite sharply. But Kate had always been as stubborn as an Irish mule and definitely not one to bow before a challenge. So she stood her ground as he growled a warning growl. 'If you don't move by yourself, then allow me to persuade you!'

It wasn't until he had taken that fatal step towards her that Kate realised the full extent of her folly. She tried to dodge away, but already he had caught her, instantly immobilising her arms at her sides with a pair of hands like solid steel pinions. The next instant his head was bending towards her and a pair of warm lips were pressing down on hers!

Shock galvanised her to the spot—this was the very last outrage she'd been expecting!—and then something quite different from shock took over. A warm sensation akin to pleasure that started on her lips then curled right down inside her. As he prised her lips apart and his tongue sought hers, warm and flicking, like a serpent's, a sensation like fire went rushing through her, seeming to ignite the blood in her veins.

An instant later, sanity came to her rescue. For the love of mercy! She had lost all reason! How could she allow this stranger to kiss her this way!

Furious, Kate tore her mouth from his to find a pair of coal-black eyes laughing down at her. 'Now will you let me pass, *señorita*?' he challenged. 'Or do I have to take even more drastic measures?'

Glory be! And what was that supposed to mean?

Wisely, Kate did not hang around to find out. Suddenly as anxious as the hapless Ramos to see this uncouth individual off the premises, she stepped smartly aside and glared at Esquerez. 'You impudent brute!' she railed ineffectually, sensing that the insult merely amused him. 'How dare you take such liberties with me! It's high time somebody taught you some manners!'

'Like who?' he demanded. 'Like you, for example?' He threw back his dark head and scowled down a challenge. 'You think you have something to teach me, do you?'

She could teach him manners—he had few enough of those!—but Kate somehow doubted she could teach him much else. There was a more than adequate fund of worldly knowledge in the black eyes that flashed down at her with such careless insolence. She had tasted some of that worldliness in that kiss of his—the memory of which made her instantly flush.

She glanced away quickly, despising her own gaucherie. 'There are definitely some gaps in your education,' she muttered.

'You think so, do you, sweet *señorita*?' His tone was mocking as with utter panache he reached out one hand to tilt her chin before she could snatch her face away. He smiled as his fingers scorched her fragile skin. 'Well, unfortunately, we'll have to skip the lessons for now.' The dark eyes held hers with impudent intimacy. 'Some other occasion, perhaps, when I'm a little less pressed for time.' He laughed softly, 'Farewell, *señorita*.' Then with a final harsh glance in Ramos's direction, that had the other man shrinking in his shoes, he turned and walked quickly across the floor and into the conveniently waiting lift.

A moment later, to the regret of no one in room, the doors closed behind him and he disappeared from sight.

The remainder of Kate's sojourn at Ramos Worldwide was something of an anti-climax after that—though, at least, she discovered, she had come to the right place. This story on which she'd pinned all her hopes actually did exist, after all.

'You're a clever young lady,' Ramos flattered her, when she'd finished explaining the purpose of her mission. 'Only a very small handful of people at the moment know about the lost tribe of Cabayan. And you're absolutely right. Ramos Worldwide have been involved from the beginning in the expedition that made the discovery. We provided the financial backing.'

He smiled across at her and added proudly, 'Basically, we're just an import-export business, but we like to do our bit for worthy causes.'

Kate had felt her heart leap with wild excitement. So the story she'd been told in a Hong Kong bar by a friendly British engineer had not, as she'd feared, been mere fanciful invention. The story of a lifetime, the answer to her prayers, was waiting for her right here in the Philippines!

But her glow of triumph was short-lived. Ramos frowned and shook his head. 'Alas, however, I must disappoint you. It is out of the question for you to visit Cabayan.'

'Why on earth not?' Kate stared at him in horror. 'Surely you're not planning to keep this discovery a secret?'

'Of course not, of course not,' Ramos assured her. 'The world has a right to know all about it.'

He smiled a faintly cautious smile. 'However, I confess, we were rather hoping to keep the Press at bay for just a little longer—just until we get ourselves better organised.' Sighing, he went on to explain, 'Cabayan is a remote and primitive place—not an easy place to get to. It would be quite impossible for someone like yourself to make the journey there alone.'

'Couldn't you provide me with a guide? Naturally, I'd be prepared to pay.'

'We have no guides free, alas, at the moment. That's what I mean when I say we're unprepared. The best I can suggest is that you meet Professor Flynn—as you know, he's in charge of the expedition—when he comes up to Manila in two weeks' time. And, should you still feel inclined to make the journey, we might even have some spare guides to lend you by then.'

Two whole weeks? She couldn't wait that long! Some other journalist might scoop the story in the meantime!

As her brain scrambled for a solution, she had a flash of inspiration. Hadn't she heard Ramos mention Cabayan in the midst of his quarrel with Esquerez? 'Don't think you can come here and start throwing your weight about—any more than you can in Cabayan!' Those were the words she'd heard him say. As Ramos stood up to show her to the door, with great delicacy, Kate enquired, 'Is that man Esquerez in any way involved in your project in Cabayan?' She paused and smiled innocently. 'I take he is *the* Esquerez of Esquerez Engineering?'

Ramos nodded. 'The very same.' Then his expression darkened to a scowl. 'Over my dead body he'll be involved in Cabayan. His only interest is in exploiting the tribe—using them as cheap labour, stealing their land from them. Esquerez, I promise you, is a greedy and wicked man.'

That was more or less what Kate had been told. But, for the moment, judging Esquerez was not what concerned her. It was with an altogether different notion in mind that she observed conversationally as they reached the office door, 'His company is based up north in Baguio, I understand.' Then she added, fishing, 'Does he have an office in Manila?'

'Only a very small one. When he's in the capital he conducts most of his business from the Manila Hotel. He has a permanent suite there. Nothing but the best.'

With a wry smile he held out his hand to shake Kate's. 'Goodbye, Miss O'Shaughnessy. I'm sorry I couldn't help you.'

But Kate was smiling as his office door clicked shut behind her and she headed on spry steps towards the lift. Mr Ramos, unwittingly, had helped her immensely. Thanks to him, she had a plan that just might save her!

At seven-thirty, on the dot, Kate walked through the main door of the Manila Hotel and into the stunningly elegant lobby.

She was looking quite different from the faintly dishevelled, heat-stricken figure of this afternoon—dressed now in a crisp white cotton shirt-dress with a tan leather belt encircling her slim waist.

On the short journey by taxi from her own hotel, she had sat ramrod straight to avoid creasing her outfit, and had taken exceedingly particular care to choose a taxi whose air-conditioning was functioning properly! For the crucial encounter that she had planned she needed to look her fighting best!

On brisk, confident steps she crossed the huge lobby with its dazzling white and gold colonnades, the heels of her sandals clicking soundlessly against the sumptuously carpeted floor, red-gold hair swinging to her shoulders, a gleam of unstoppable Irish determination shining from her bright green eyes. Esquerez didn't know it yet, but he was about to have a visitor!

She approached the reception desk. 'I'm a guest of Mr de Esquerez, but I'm afraid I've forgotten the number of his suite.' Then, as the receptionist provided her with this vital information, Kate confided coquettishly, 'Don't bother to ring up. I want to surprise him.'

The receptionist smiled and made a quick check of the keys. 'You should find him in his suite. Take the elevator to the third floor.'

So, she had timed her visit perfectly! He had not gone out. Kate headed for the lifts on confident steps. Perhaps now he would do her the further service of providing the assistance that Ramos could not. He didn't know it, of course, but he owed her one, and perhaps he could help her get to Cabayan!

Up on the third floor reigned that opulent hush one tended only to encounter in the very best hotels. Following the arrows, Kate walked briskly along the corridor, aware that her heart was beating ever faster as the adrenalin began to flow.

This encounter, she sensed, might well provide difficult—from what she had seen of him Esquerez was a difficult man—but it might also prove to be the solution to her problems. For that she was prepared to face the tiger in his lair!

She reached the door at last and paused to brace herself—took a deep breath, straightened her shoulders and shook her hair back from her face. Then, resolutely, she raised her hand and tapped twice, loudly, with the back of her knuckles.

There was no immediate response. Was he out, after all? Perhaps he had forgotten to hand in his key? Frowning, she raised her hand to knock again, but before her knuckles made contact with the paintwork the door sprang open and she was presented with a vision that made her step back hurriedly.

Esquerez, yes, but in no state for visitors!

He was dressed in nothing but a skimpy blue towel that had been hastily wrapped around his waist—and, somehow, in this state of semi-naked splendour he seemed even taller and broader than she had remembered.

She had evidently wrenched him from the shower. The jet-black hair, glistening like satin, was dripping droplets of water over his shoulders and chest. Droplets which gathered into tiny rivulets which then coursed almost lovingly down the bronzed, manly contours, their progress slowing slightly as they encountered the crisp black hairs that complemented his chest then ran in a thin dark line down his stomach to disappear beneath the towel.

The state of his physique beyond the border of the towel Kate preferred to let remain a mystery. Resolutely, she kept her eyes fixed on his face.

The black gaze was harsh and not at all encouraging as he pushed his wet hair back from his forehead. His mouth straightened into a line of impatience. 'You!' he snarled irritably, recognising her instantly. 'What do you want?' he demanded curtly.

Undeterred, Kate stared back boldly. 'I've come to see you,' she informed him coolly, softening her statement with an enigmatic smile.

He straightened a fraction. 'Have you, indeed?' Then, with a flicker of annoyance, he went on to enquire grandly, 'Have you any idea who I am?'

Kate frowned a little, not quite comprehending, yet somewhat impressed in spite of herself by his easy ability to retain total dignity while dressed in nothing but a towel!

He did not wait for her to answer his question; instead he answered it himself, informing her, still in that grand tone, 'I am Vittorio Felipe Salvador de Esquerez—and, as such, *señorita*, I do not make a habit of entertaining uninvited young women in my room!'

What utter arrogance! Kate glared straight back at him. He had evidently misinterpreted that enigmatic smile!

'And I am Katharine Brigid Mhaire O'Shaughnessy!' If he insisted on bandying around pedigrees, he wasn't the only one with a fine string of names! 'And as such,' she went on crisply to enlighten him, 'I do not make a habit of knocking on strange men's doors! I am here for a very good reason. And not,' she added, flushing with irritation, 'for the reason that you seem to think.'

'Oh, no?' The black eyes gleamed wickedly down at her, apparently more amused than angered by her reaction. 'Are you trying to tell me that you have not come here in order to continue our earlier encounter where we left off?' He smiled a deliberately disbelieving smile. 'You should have rung me, *señorita*. We could have arranged a more convenient time.'

From the insolent curve of the bow-shaped lips, Kate could tell that he was deliberately baiting her. Yet at the same time, too, she sensed with a flutter, his words were not spoken entirely in jest—which was why she proceeded to fix him with her most withering look.

'I'm afraid, Señor de Esquerez, you couldn't be more wrong. I came here for nothing so unpleasant nor so frivolous.' The very thought gave her goosebumps of sheer horror! 'I came here in order to talk business with you. I'm sorry if I caught you at an inconvenient moment.'

Vittorio Felipe Salvador de Esquerez leaned his magnificent, bronzed body against the door-jamb. 'Business, you say?' he repeated, eyeing her. 'What manner of business could you and I possibly have?'

'That's what I've come here to discuss. And I don't intend to discuss it out in the hallway.'

He shrugged and looked down at her with eyes as black as jet. 'So, where do you suggest we discuss it, Katharine Brigid Mhaire O'Shaughnessy?'

'Perhaps, once you're dressed, you could spare me half an hour and we could discuss it downstairs in the coffee shop or at the bar.' Originally, she had thought they might be able to talk civilly in his suite, but civility, quite clearly, was not one of his strong points. She would, she reckoned, for all manner of reasons, prefer to confront him in a public place.

But he was not about to comply with her wishes. 'Once I've dressed, I regret, I shall be going straight out to a dinner appointment.' Despite his polite words, not a shadow of regret was discernible in his strong-boned face. 'Unless you, also, are a guest tonight at the American ambassador's, I see little opportunity for us to talk.'

Damn him! Kate glared at him, keeping a tight rein on her temper. The man was pompous and infuriating. She was tempted just to turn round and walk away. But he could be her only hope of getting to Cabayan. So, instead, she enquired politely, 'What about tomorrow?'

'Tomorrow, alas, I shall not be here. Urgent business demands my presence elsewhere.'

Almost simultaneously, her spirits rose and fell. Could this urgent business of his possibly be in Cabayan? If so, it was essential she talk with him before he left. 'Surely you could spare me a couple of minutes of your time?' As much as it went against the grain, she laced her words with a soft note of pleading. 'What I want to talk to you about is extremely important.'

Unmoved, he looked back at her. 'Important to whom?'

'To me, and to the people I work for—and I promise you there would be something in it for you.'

'Is that a fact?' He regarded her slowly, the dark eyes sliding down from her face to scrutinise with expert thoroughness every intimate detail of her slender shape, making her feel as though it was she and not he who was standing there half-naked in only a towel. 'You have me curious now,' he confessed. 'What could a girl like you possibly have to offer me—apart from the obvious, of course?'

Then, as she hesitated, momentarily uncertain of how to respond, he stepped back into the room and told her. 'You can come and put your case to me while I'm dressing. That, I'm afraid, is my final offer.'

As invitations went, it did not appeal greatly. No, thank you, was right on the tip of Kate's tongue. But she hesitated and pleaded again, 'Couldn't you just give me ten minutes downstairs?'

'When I say final, I mean final, *señorita*.' To her horror, the door began to close.

'No, wait!' she blustered, taking an anxious step forward. Hadn't she decided he might be her only hope? And she absolutely *had* to get to Cabayan. On this story depended her future and Liam's.

And yet... The more she looked at him, the more she felt disposed to hesitate. There was something about this man that disturbed her deeply and she could not quite analyse what it was.

'Well?' He was waiting, the door half ajar. 'I'll count up to three and then we'll discuss it no more.' He regarded her indecisive face. '*Uno...*' he began.

As she stood there, frozen, the door closed another fraction. '*Dos...*'

It closed a little more.

'*Tre——*'

But he did not quite manage to finish the final *tres*. With the air of a combatant going into battle— fists clenched, chin up and a prayer in her heart— Kate had walked smartly past him, into the room.

CHAPTER TWO

ONCE Kate was inside the tiger's lair the door closed behind her with an ominous click.

Kate swung round to face the towel-clad Esquerez, anxious to make her position quite clear. 'Kindly remember that I'm your guest,' she challenged, intrepidly holding the burning black gaze. 'You invited me in here, don't forget. So, I expect to be treated with the courtesy and respect that is the right of any guest.'

A flicker of amusement touched the bow-shaped lips. 'So, you seek, once again, to teach me manners? Well, don't worry, Katharine Brigid Mhaire O'Shaughnessy, I come from an ancient and honourable family. I have no need of lessons from you on matters pertaining to social etiquette.'

Regarding the first half of his claim, Kate had heard as much. By all accounts he was directly descended from one of the illustrious Spanish grandee families which had ruled the Philippines for three hundred years. That was before the Americans took over briefly and the country gained independence in 1946.

Kate, however, was not unduly impressed. He might have blue blood flowing through his veins, but he had the rough manners of a peasant!

She gave a scoffing laugh. 'You could have fooled me! I didn't see much evidence of your acquaintance with social etiquette at our meeting this afternoon!'

Instantly, she regretted her tart reminder. The black eyes suddenly twinkled with devilment as they looked down at her and he replied, 'Surely one is permitted the occasional small lapse—particularly in the face of such irresistible provocation?' His smile broadened shamelessly, showing those wickedly white teeth. 'If you want to keep me on my best behaviour, you must take care, *señorita*, not to provoke me again.'

Was that a threat? Kate did not like threats. She looked back at him boldly. 'Where I come from a gentleman is always on his best behaviour. He does not drop his standards under any provocation.'

'Here the rules are different.' The black eyes challenged her. 'You must play by the rules—or accept the consequences.'

To Kate's intense irritation she flushed a little at his deliberate reference to that kiss. She tilted her chin at him. 'I shall try to remember that.' Then she added, eyeing him with a show of distaste, 'Fortunately, it should not be too difficult. The consequences were so unpleasant.'

'You found them so? I cannot agree. Myself, I found them rather enjoyable.'

He was loving every minute of this verbal skirmish. The black eyes were sparkling mischievously down at her. But the way the conversation was heading was making Kate distinctly uncomfortable.

She folded her arms across her chest. 'I didn't come here to engage in empty chit-chat. As I've told you already, I have something I wish to discuss with you.'

'Empty chit-chat can be most revealing. Too bad. I was just beginning to get to know you.'

Such presumption! 'I doubt that very much.' But she bit back the observation that she, for her part, had not the faintest desire to get to know him. She was here, after all, to ask him a favour. For the moment it was in her interests to be polite.

Kate uncrossed her arms and softened her expression. 'I would be most grateful if we could get down to business.'

They were standing in the drawing-room of the suite, a finely furnished room, tasteful and elegant. Esquerez shrugged. 'Very well, then.' Without further ado he turned smartly on his heel and headed for the doorway that led into the bedroom. 'Come!' he commanded, 'Follow me.'

Kate remained standing right where she was. 'If you don't mind, I'll stay in here.'

Esquerez paused in the open doorway. 'Suit yourself.' He smiled an amused smile. 'But it beats me how you hope to a conduct a conversation with me in one room and you in another.'

It beat her, too, once she paused to consider it. 'But you have to get dressed,' she offered lamely.

He shook his dark head and regarded her curiously. 'What's the matter, Katharine Brigid Mhaire O'Shaughnessy? Have you never seen a man naked before?'

Maybe she had and maybe she hadn't, but either way it was none of his damned business! She regarded him boldly. 'I came here to speak, not to be subjected to some sort of strip-tease.'

He smiled at her mockingly. 'Don't worry, *señorita*. I have many faults, but you can take my word for it, exhibitionism is not one of them. I shall make myself decent in the bathroom before we embark on our little tête-à-tête. You may come through and make yourself comfortable in the meanwhile—without fear, I guarantee, of being molested.'

He would molest her at his peril, Kate thought sharply, as she followed him through into the opulent bedroom. No man took unwanted liberties with Kate O'Shaughnessy! Yet she could not deny, regarding his threat of a strip-tease, that were he in fact to go ahead with it she would be unlikely to behold a more perfect specimen.

Every visible inch of him was a pleasure to the eye. From the sinuous, rippling back with its magnificent mahogany shoulders to the well-turned calves beneath the hip-moulding towel, he had a body the beauty of which could bring tears to female eyes. He even appeared to have handsome feet, that carried him with the supple spring of an athlete, and the hand that paused on the bathroom doorknob, as he turned round briefly to glance her way, was long-fingered and strong, yet sensitively proportioned.

Damn him for his physical perfection, Kate thought sourly, as, with a wave of that self-same elegant hand, he bade her, 'Take a seat. I'll only be a couple of minutes—then we can get down to this business of yours.'

Kate sat on the first chair that came to hand as he disappeared into the bathroom and closed the door. And she couldn't help wondering, as she was left alone, what Liam would make of Vittorio de Esquerez.

At the thought of her younger brother Kate's heart squeezed within her. For Liam, whose wise and canny insights she invariably relied upon in her assessments of men, was a great deal more than an infallible judge of character. He was the most precious person in the whole wide world to her. And, of course, he was also the reason she was here.

Dear Liam. She frowned and shook her head. If she failed in this mission, if she didn't make it to Cabayan, if she was forced to leave the Philippines without her story, Liam's entire future would be in jeopardy.

For, if she failed to get this story, her own job would be on the line, and that, in turn, would affect her brother.

Her thoughts were interrupted as the bathroom door opened and Esquerez came striding into the room. He paused for a moment, his dark eyes on her, unaware of the anxieties in her heart. 'So. Speak your piece,' he charged without preamble. 'Kindly do me the favour of explaining why you've come here.'

He was dressed only in a pair of slim dark trousers, a black crocodile belt hanging loosely around his waist, and as Kate glanced up into his face she had a sudden searing insight into what Liam would have to say about him.

His judgement, she sensed, would not be favourable—though not in the humorously scathing way that he invariably wrote off her boyfriends. No, she decided, he would despise Esquerez as one of those arrogant individuals who had, always had

had and always would have everything their hearts desired. And he would remind her that such people dispensed favours reluctantly. They held on tightly to what was theirs and demanded coldly weighed payment for every good turn done.

Kate smiled to herself knowingly. She would keep that in mind. She must ask no favours of him. Instead, she must bargain.

In a clear voice now she answered his question. 'I've come to the Philippines on a very particular mission—one in which you yourself, I believe, have an interest. I was hoping we might be able to co-operate with one another.'

He had crossed on bare feet to the tall mirrored wall cupboard and lifted out a shirt while she was speaking. His back to her now, addressing her mirrored reflection, he slid the crisp white garment from its hanger and, in one sinuous movement, slipped it on. His tone barbed and lightly sceptical, he put to her, 'Before we start talking about co-operation, *señorita*, perhaps you would care to clarify what manner of mission you are talking about?'

Calmly, Kate met his reflected glance. 'It concerns the lost tribe of Cabayan,' she informed him.

He turned round then to look at her directly. 'The lost tribe of Cabayan?' he repeated.

Kate nodded. 'You know about them, of course? I understand you have some interest in the tribe yourself?'

Esquerez crossed to a set of drawers by the bed and lifted out a pair of black silk socks. Then he sat down on the edge of the vast quilted bedspread and unhurriedly proceeded to pull them on. He

glanced up at Kate through thick black lashes, his
tone faintly guarded as he told her, 'Yes, I do indeed
have an interest in the tribe.' Then he stood up
abruptly, before she could answer. 'No doubt you
gained this information from Ramos?'

Kate flinched a little as he took an impatient step
towards her, the unbuttoned shirt flying open as he
moved, revealing that bronzed and deeply muscled
chest. 'It came up by the way,' she answered guiltily.
'We were not discussing your business, if that's
what you're thinking.'

'That's a relief.' His tone was sarcastic. He
walked past her to the mirror above the chest of
drawers, doing up the buttons of his shirt as he
went. Then, with unexpected venom, he informed
her over his shoulder, 'That piece of vermin knows
nothing about my business, so it is not within his
powers to discuss it with anyone.'

Almost contemptuously, he tucked his shirt into
his trousers and fastened the gilt-buckled crocodile
belt. Then, with an impatient gesture, he pulled
open a drawer and lifted out a black bow tie, raised
the collar of his shirt and slipped the tie around his
neck. 'So, what does this mission of yours entail,
and what manner of co-operation were you envis-
aging between us?'

As he spoke, in clipped and hostile syllables, Kate
was aware of her own hostility leaping up at least
a dozen notches. This was the man whose all-
powerful company, or at least its local Hong Kong
branch, had effectively scuppered her last as-
signment for *Deadline*.

She had gone to the crown colony with every intention of scooping herself a front cover story,

something she needed badly if she was going to hang on to her job. What she had finished up with was a mundane effort that would end up tucked away on one of the minor inside pages—and all because one of the key protagonists in her story, Esquerez Engineering, had refused her an interview. No proper reason had been given. She had simply been told, 'We don't speak to the Press.'

Kate felt her heart sink a little at the memory. If it was company policy not to co-operate with journalists, she was going to have a hard time persuading its chairman to help her. And yet she was determined to do it.

She paused for a moment, her eyes on his deft fingers as they swiftly executed an impeccable bow in his tie. 'Señor de Esquerez,' she began a little hesitantly, like one stepping barefoot on to broken glass, 'perhaps I should start off by telling you something about myself.' A more personal approach might soothe his antagonism and make him more amenable to her ultimate proposal. 'Señor de Esquerez,' she continued, 'I'm a——'

But before she could add 'journalist', he cut right through her. 'You're an associate of Ramos's. That's all I need to know about you.'

'You're wrong, I'm not an associate of Ramos's.'

He eyed her in the mirror. 'Then what were you doing in his office?'

'I went to seek his help, but he was unable to assist me—and that is why I've come to see you.' Even as she said it, Kate cursed herself inwardly. That had sounded as though she was asking a favour. She corrected herself swiftly. 'I have a proposal to put to you.'

'So you said.' Esquerez smiled harshly in the mirror. 'But why, *señorita*, should I be interested in your proposal? A proposal that Ramos has already turned down.'

'He didn't turn me down.' Kate's tone was impatient. 'He was unable to co-operate. That is rather different.'

'Unable to co-operate. A subtle distinction. But, then, our good friend Ramos is nothing if not subtle.'

Which was a great deal more than could be said for Esquerez, Kate was thinking with mounting irritation. The way he was picking up on everything she said was quite clearly intended to be obstructive.

But as she was about to rebuke him, he changed tack again. 'I believe you were on the point of telling me about yourself—before I so rudely interrupted you . . .'

Kate glared at his amused and arrogant reflection. He was an impossible man to deal with, impossible to get the better of. How would she ever be able to persuade him?

As she watched him, he smiled again. 'Continue. I'm waiting.'

And it was that smile perhaps, so openly taunting, that was responsible for what happened next.

Kate took a deep breath. 'I was about to explain,' she began, 'that I'm a . . .' As before, she had fully intended to be honest. 'Journalist' was the word she had been about to say next. But as the lie popped from nowhere into her head, she found herself saying instead, '. . . an anthropologist.'

Kate bit her lip, faintly shocked at herself. She had not known she had it in her to be so downright devious. And she was hovering on the point of retracting the lie when Esquerez turned round to look at her, for once without hostility.

'An anthropologist?' he repeated with interest. 'Who do you work for?'

She could not throw away this unexpected advantage. She looked straight at him. 'I'm still studying—in London. In fact, I'm working on my thesis.' Suddenly the lies were tripping from her lips with the gay abandon of lemmings jumping off a cliff. 'I'm doing research on the social structure of isolated tribes,' she finished, genuinely awe-struck by her performance.

And Esquerez, she noted with pleasure, also appeared to be mildly impressed. 'Hence your interest in the tribe of Cabayan? I take it it's your intention to include them in your studies?'

'Exactly.' Kate nodded and watched with growing excitement as, with a thoughtful expression, he crossed back to the wardrobe and lifted out a pair of shiny black shoes. Clearly, he was less hostile towards anthropologists than journalists. That was a pretty smart move she had made!

He slid his feet into the shoes and raised black eyes to glance across at her. 'That's all very interesting,' he said, 'but what has it to do with me? What's this very important business proposition that you were talking about?'

Kay licked her lips that had suddenly gone dry. Perhaps, she was almost daring to think, persuading him might not prove to be so difficult after all.

Still, with a man like Esquerez, one must never assume, so she began now on a cautious note. 'I came over here to the Philippines hoping that Mr Ramos might be able to help me organise my trip down to Cabayan... But, unfortunately, he tells me he has no spare guides right now. I would try to make it on my own, but Ramos told me that would be inadvisable.'

Esquerez allowed himself an amused little laugh as he lifted down his dinner-jacket from its hanger. 'At least, for once in his life, he was telling the truth. It would be *most* inadvisable, I'd say. The terrain between here and Cabayan is mostly jungle, with no proper roads. Though it's only a matter of a few hundred miles, it's a journey that can take several days.' He slid on the jacket and adjusted the lapels. 'I'd put your chances of making it on your own at least ten thousand to one against.'

Discouraging odds. Kate pursed her lips and watched as he crossed to the dressing-table mirror and quickly brushed his still-damp hair.

He looked extraordinarily arresting in the dark dinner-suit, she found herself acknowledging as she watched his broad back. And there was no sign now of the undisciplined savage whom she had met this morning in Ramos's office. The man before her was pure aristocrat, from his sleek head right down to his shiny black shoes. The wild jackal had transformed himself into a panther.

And there was something a little unsettling about this two-sided quality of his. It made it frustratingly impossible to pin him down.

He turned suddenly to look at her. 'Why not wait for the professor, your fellow anthropologist? He'll be returning to Manila in a couple of weeks' time. He could take you with him to meet the tribe when he returns.'

Kate shook her head. 'I can't wait that long. I have pressing business back in England.' Then, weighing her words carefully, she picked up her argument. 'You were saying that you yourself have an interest in the lost tribe.' She paused for a millisecond, her heart beating within her. 'Am I right in thinking you might be planning a visit to Cabayan?'

The crossbow-shaped lips curved enigmatically. 'I may be,' he replied.

'Is that where you're going tomorrow?' Kate pressed, suddenly certain that it was.

Esquerez slipped a slim crocodile wallet and a gold Cartier pen into his inside jacket pocket. Then, strapping on a pure gold, wafer-thin Rolex, he turned round to look at her. 'Why do you ask?'

'Well, I was wondering . . .' This was the moment of truth. 'I was wondering if, since I have no other way of getting there, you might consider taking me with you?'

'Were you?' He raised one straight dark eyebrow. 'Well, you can stop wondering right away. The answer, *señorita*, is very simple. No, I would not for one moment consider it.'

She had phrased her request badly, Kate realised belatedly. Once again it had sounded as though she was asking a favour. She hurried now to put that impression right. 'Naturally, I wouldn't expect you to do it for nothing. I could make it worth your while.'

Esquerez paused. 'Ah, yes, of course, I had forgotten. You said at the start there'd be something in it for me.'

Instantly, Kate's spirits lifted. She had judged him correctly. He would help her for a price. But the price of such a man would be far from bargain basement—so, bracing herself, she named a sum far in excess of her professional budget. 'That's what I would be prepared to pay you if you'll take me to Cabayan.'

For one long, agonised moment he regarded her in silence, the razor-sharp gaze darkly inscrutable. Then, without a flicker of emotion, he spoke. 'Sorry,' he said, and turned away.

Kate rose to her feet, her heart suddenly pounding. She couldn't let him turn her down! Boldly, she doubled her original figure and announced it to his implacable back. So what if she had to dip into her own pocket? She absolutely *had* to get that story.

'Well, what do you say?' She waited anxiously, hardly daring to hear his answer.

When it came, at least, it was plain and unequivocal. '*Señorita*, you misjudge me. I am not remotely interested in your money. Not if you were to offer me the British Crown jewels would I consider for one moment taking you with me.'

He swung round to look at her, his head lifting imperiously, every splendid sinew bristling with pride. 'I would suggest that you're wasting your time here, Miss O'Shaughnessy. You would be well advised to just go back to England and find yourself some other tribe to study.'

'But why?' She took an impulsive step towards him, her tone tight with emotion as she sought to win him round. 'Even if you're not interested in the money—and I apologise if I offended you— why not let me come along with you? I promise you I would be no trouble! I might even be of some assistance.'

He laughed then, a mocking, dismissive laugh and shook his head slowly, as though addressing a small child. 'You think so, do you, sweet *señorita*? In a place like Cabayan, I fear, you would be more than just trouble. Your presence would be a down-right and dangerous liability!'

'So, that *is* where you're going!' He had as good as admitted it! '*Please*, Señor de Esquerez, take me along!'

'Never!' His tone was final. He snapped up his wrist and glanced at his watch. 'I have already wasted too much time on this nonsense. I shall be late for my appointment. It's time for you to leave.'

So, just like that, he was casually dismissing her and callously squashing all her precious hopes! But too much depended on this mission. She couldn't give in to him just like that. As he started to move round her, as though to lead her to the door, she side-stepped quickly, blocking his path.

'I really wish you would reconsider,' she urged. 'You have nothing to fear by taking me along. I'm fit and healthy, I'm in good physical shape and I'm very good at looking after myself.' Perhaps his reservations were simply based on the fear of having a namby-pamby woman on his hands!

He took a leisurely moment to check out her claims, the sharp black eyes travelling her slim, vital form, the swell of her breasts beneath the soft white shirtdress, the neat curve of her waist, the womanly hips. 'I have no complaints with what I see,' he agreed, as his gaze returned at last to her face. 'It all looks in remarkably fine order to me. I congratulate you, Katharine Brigid Mhaire O'Shaughnessy.'

Kate ignored the wolfish flicker in his eyes and went on to insist, her tone persuasive, 'I could make myself useful to you on the trip. As an able-bodied female, I could do the cooking and things.'

'Oh, yes?' His tone purred with sudden interest. 'And what other little services, apart from cooking, would you care to provide with that able and desirable young body of yours?'

That brought her up short. Kate made to step back, but Esquerez had already taken a step forward. All at once, one hand was on her waist, the other reaching out to lace her hair. And she could feel her scalp burst into flames as the black eyes burned down into hers.

'Eh, *señorita*? I'm waiting for your answer.'

It was the unexpectedness and the arrogant boldness of the move that caught her momentarily unawares, just as before in Ramos's office. Immobile, she stared back at him, as he purred again, 'Come, *señorita*. Don't be modest. What else would you do for me if I took you along?'

Yet there was another less palatable explanation for her response—or, rather, for her lack of one. Although she would never have confessed it, not even under torture, there was something quite overpoweringly pleasurable about the virile hard warmth of his body against hers. She had never felt her nerve-ends tingle so deliciously, nor her heart beat within her at such a giddy rate.

He leaned closer, the dark eyes mean and ravenous, those curved crossbow lips of his perilously near. And, to her shame, Kate found herself half hoping he might kiss her before she had the chance to break away. But, instead, all at once, almost roughly, he released her. 'Sorry, *señorita*, I have no time to taste your wares.'

What utter bare-faced insolence! Kate glared at him in fury—though, in truth, she was uncertain what had sparked her sudden outrage. His initial assault on her or his ultimate rejection? The former, of course, she told herself firmly, as she rounded on Esquerez, green eyes flashing. 'So much for your gentlemanly assurances that you treat your guests with courtesy and respect! That was one of the most insulting displays of bad manners that I have ever encountered in my life!'

'Then you have been fortunate indeed, *señorita*.' He continued to stand over her without a whisper of remorse. 'A young woman with a penchant for deliberate provocation as blatant as yours is asking for trouble.' He paused. 'I warned you, did I not?' Then, when she failed to answer, he continued, 'If you are not careful, one day you may have the misfortune to run into someone who is more ruthless and less of a gentleman than I.' The black eyes ravished her with a look of contempt. 'And then you will be required to deliver the goods.'

Kate would gladly have slapped him across his arrogant face had not the thought of further physical contact with him suddenly appalled her. How dared he insinuate that she was some kind of tease? *He* was the one with ideas in his head—and a pair of far-too-ready hands, and lips! Though this time, at least, he had kept the latter to himself!

'You——! You——!' Incoherently, she spluttered, not even certain what she wanted to say. But, ignoring her totally, he had crossed to the door, making a bridge with his arm as he held it open and, with a nod of his head, invited her to pass through.

'Goodbye, Miss O'Shaughnessy,' he intoned curtly. 'I wish I could say it's been a pleasure meeting you, but my innate honesty precludes such a lie.'

Innate honesty! That was a laugh!

She glared at him, none the less far from amused, hating the insolent mockery in his eyes. 'Likewise!' was all she could think of to say, her quick Irish wit momentarily deserting her.

He was also the first man ever to have had *that* effect. And, somehow, that was almost more unsettling than his previous, more physical, first!

'I think you'll find there's a London flight tomorrow morning. Your wisest move would be to book a seat on it.' He stood there, arrogance personified, his hand still propped against the door, inviting her to pass beneath.

She would have to duck slightly to make her exit, Kate calculated with a glance. His arm was arranged at precisely the correct angle to inflict this ultimate humiliation.

But that was going just a little too far! He had misjudged her if he thought she would let him off with that!

'Goodbye, Señor de Esquerez,' she answered evenly, as she crossed unhurriedly to stand in front of him, her green eyes travelling with pointed hostility to the strategically placed arm impeding her way.

He did not move, nor did his arm budge an inch, and she could feel the dark eyes fixed on her face, daring her to see out her bluff.

Just swallow your pride and duck, her brain told her. For sweet heaven's sake, don't provoke him again!

But something stronger than plain common sense was urging her more loudly not to back down. In cool, careful syllables she told him, 'If you don't mind ... I'm waiting.'

'Waiting?' The bow of his mouth curved wickedly. One black eyebrow arched in mock incomprehension.

'Yes, waiting, Señor de Esquerez—for you to remove your arm so I can get past.'

Two pairs of eyes, one emerald, one ebony, snapped together like castanets. Then each paused for a moment to take the measure of the other, neither prepared to concede an inch.

The moment seemed to go on forever, then, in a magnificent parody of gallantry, as though he had suddenly tired of the game, Esquerez abruptly dropped his arm from the door and, bowing deeply, invited her to pass.

'My honour as a gentleman compels me ... *Señorita, por favor.*'

Kate wasted not a second in making her exit, but she went with perfect dignity, her head held high.

She had made her point and now she was anxious to be gone.

He made no effort to impede her. *'Adios, señorita,'* she heard him murmur, that familiar mocking ring of bravura in his voice.

Kate did not turn to look at him. 'Goodbye,' she repeated.

And may our paths never cross again, she was praying.

Kate went straight back to her own hotel, then took a shower and ordered some dinner from room service. And a big juicy steak and a carafe of wine proved an excellent antidote to the execrable Esquerez. But her principal problem remained unresolved. How was she going to get to Cabayan?

She glanced at her watch. It was lunchtime back home. Perhaps she could catch Derek, her editor, before he went out.

Her timing, luckily, was perfect. 'He's free,' his secretary told her, putting her through.

A moment later, after an exchange of greetings, she was reluctantly confessing, 'I'm having a few problems.' She went on to explain about her encounter with Ramos and her subsequent disastrous meeting with Esquerez. 'It's beginning to look as though I'm stuck in Manila until Professor Flynn returns.'

There was a thoughtful pause as Derek took in this news, then she could almost see him shake his head as he told her, 'I'm sorry, Kate, but I can't have you waiting around idly for two weeks in Manila. If you can't find a way to get the story, then you'll just have to get the first plane back.'

It was more or less the reaction she'd been expecting, but she felt a plummet of disappointment all the same. 'But, Derek, it's such a fantastic story,' she wheedled. 'And once Flynn comes back I'll probably be able to arrange something.'

'No can do.' Derek was immovable. 'There are plenty of other stories waiting to be written. Sorry, Kate, we need you back here.' Then, hearing her groan of disappointment, he added encouragingly, 'This Esquerez chap sounds like your best bet. Why don't you have another go at him?'

Kate's spirits crumpled at the thought. Never in a million years! she vowed. But, before she could answer, Derek went on, 'Let me know tomorrow if you're coming back. If I don't hear from you I'll assume you've managed to fix something up. I'll get in touch with one of our Asia-based photographers and you can brief him on the pics you want when you get back to Manila.' He broke off abruptly. 'Got to go now, Kate. Just do your best, and keep in touch.'

As Kate laid down the phone she felt like weeping. That was her very last hope gone. Now she would never get the story that could have saved her job and her brother's future.

Damn Esquerez! It was all his fault!

So there was nothing for it now but to go back to England with her tail between her legs. She breakfasted glumly in her room next morning, studying the flight times without enthusiasm, then picked up the phone to make a reservation.

But at the very last minute, as the receptionist answered, something short-circuited in her head.

Instead of asking to be put through to the airport, she heard herself request, 'Kindly get me the Manila Hotel.'

There was a buzz and a click as her request was granted, and, a moment later, as she was connected, Kate demanded, clearly and calmly, 'I want to speak to Señor de Esquerez.'

It was folly. Sheer madness. What had possessed her? Her heart was hammering like a piston in her chest.

And it was hard to tell if she was relieved or sorry, as she was informed politely by the receptionist, 'I'm sorry, but Señor de Esquerez has gone out.' A pause as Kate was about to lay down the receiver, then, just in time, the receptionist added, 'However, he left a message to say he's lunching at the Yacht Club, just in case there were any important messages.'

Kate swallowed. 'Thank you.' Then she laid down the phone. It was clear now what she had to do.

She took a taxi to the Yacht Club just before one and marched through the gates past the security guard with all the careless panache of a lifelong member. She would catch Esquerez off guard and have one more go at him, she had decided, just as Derek had suggested. Though she did not rate her chances of success very highly, it was the one and only hope she had left.

The club restaurant was immediately visible, even without entering the Yacht Club building itself. On the wooden veranda on its sea-facing side a row of white-clothed tables were set out, with a clear, uninterrupted view over the magnificent blue waters of Manila Bay. And there, as large as life, at one of the tables, sat the very man she had come to see!

There was only one snag. He was not alone. Seated right beside him, and apparently entranced by his conversation, sat a stunningly beautiful dark-haired girl.

Curse and damnation! Kate swore to herself. Rashly, she had assumed he would be alone, and the fact that he wasn't was a serious blow.

How could she approach him when he was in the company of this girl? It would be far too simple for him to put her off. For it was clear that the girl was no casual acquaintance. There was a quite radiant aura of intimacy between them. Kate would feel highly uncomfortable intruding on their private tête-à-tête.

Pondering on what her next move should be, she took refuge from the sun beneath a shady tree and reflected briefly on the follies of her sex. This dark-haired beauty, whoever she was, must be mad to risk tangling with a man like Esquerez!

But that was the girl's problem! She had problems of her own—for instance, what the devil was she going to do now?

Even as she searched in vain for an answer, she saw Esquerez summon one of the waiters to his table—and out of simple curiosity, unaware that fate was about to supply the solution to her problem, Kate stood very still and watched the scene.

With a few brief words, Esquerez had dropped what looked like a set of keys into the waiter's hand. Kate continued to watch as the waiter turned away and headed off down the veranda, then disappeared from sight for a moment, before emerging through the main door, just across from her tree.

With quick steps he strode obliviously past her, heading for the car park at one side, and came to a halt almost immediately alongside a dusty white Nissan Patrol. As he stuck one of the keys in the door—she had been right about that!—Kate put two and two together and shook her head. Wasn't it just typical of the arrogant Esquerez to send a waiter to fetch something from his car, rather than make the journey himself?

But it was just at that moment that the waiter made a slip, the consequences of which were destined to reach wide and far. As he lifted a package from the front seat and slammed the car door shut, the keys dropped from the lock on to the ground. Evidently distracted by the occurrence, the waiter stooped to retrieve them—then walked away, quite forgetting to relock the door behind him.

Kate waited until he had disappeared back inside the restaurant again before darting out from behind her tree and hurrying over to the Nissan Patrol. It had to belong to Esquerez, rather than to the girl, she reckoned. A great big jeep-like, four-wheel-drive contraption, it fitted perfectly with his macho image. And, what was more, she noted, her interest growing, it was quite clearly kitted out for a journey.

Stowed in the back, among a clutter of bags, she spied what looked like a rolled-up tent and a couple of boxes of cooking utensils. Exactly the sort of stuff he would need if he was going to Cabayan!

Kate's heart did a triple jump of excitement. He *was* going to Cabayan! She was sure of it now! At the very same instant she knew beyond a doubt why fate had brought her to this place.

Not to talk to him. Not to persuade him with words. But to present him with a *fait accompli*.

With a trembling hand, she pulled open the door. Whether he liked it or not, she was going with him!

CHAPTER THREE

BY THE time she finally heard footsteps approaching, a little less than two hours later, Kate was on the verge of abandoning her strategy and escaping from her self-imposed prison cell.

She had wedged herself in the back of the Nissan, between the rolled-up tent and the cooking utensils, pulling a green plaid travelling rug carefully over her so that she was completely hidden. With any luck, Esquerez wouldn't twig her presence until they were well on their way to Cabayan! And by then, surely, she was gambling, it wouldn't be worth his while to bring her all the way back again.

But what she hadn't reckoned on was the unspeakable torture of waiting for him in the car!

The trouble was that the Philippine sun that had raised the temperature to one hundred in the shade was beating down on the unprotected Nissan with the merciless wrath of the flames of hell. In spite of her efforts to fan herself with her hand, the experience of being shut up in that steamy interior resembled nothing so much as being barbecued alive!

I'll give it another half-hour, she'd decided stoically, loath to abandon this, her only chance. And, as fate would have it, minutes short of her deadline, she heard the welcome sound of Esquerez's voice.

She grimaced wryly beneath the blanket, making an effort to keep statue-still. What a subtle irony it was that she should feel pleased to hear those arrogant tones!

The conversation was being conducted in Spanish. Kate couldn't understand a word. But she could make out a husky female voice responding and deduced that he was talking to his lady-friend. Poor, benighted female, Kate thought beneath her blanket, picturing the sophisticated-looking creature she had seen sitting at his table. Pity help her if she's at all seriously involved with him!

Then, at last, came an exchange that even Kate could decipher. *'Adios, querida.'* Vittorio's voice, finally saying his farewells.

There was a short pause—an embrace, Kate fondly imagined—then came the dark-haired young woman's reply.

'Vaya con Dios. Buen viaje.' May God go with you. Have a safe journey.

Then another short pause as a car door slammed, then a roar as the car engine sprang into life. A moment later came the crunch of tyres and a final greeting.

'Adios! Adios!'

Kate sighed with relief as footsteps came towards her, then a key grated uselessly in the lock. A soft curse, as he realised the door had been left open, then she heard him climb up into the driver's seat.

Her heart leapt with delight as he switched on the engine. Her ploy had worked! He hadn't noticed her! Then a moment later she almost jumped up to thank him as he turned on the air-conditioning full blast!

Within minutes, as they turned out through the gates of the Yacht Club and headed through the traffic on to Roxas Boulevard, Kate began to feel half human again. She lifted a corner of the blanket and breathed in deeply, daring to snatch a glance at the handsome dark profile, as he drove swiftly towards the outskirts of Manila, oblivious of the stowaway crouched at his back.

For the moment she had tricked him, Kate thought triumphantly, settling herself more comfortably in her secret corner. But she was wise enough to know her triumph was only temporary. The moment of reckoning was still to come.

Kate was jolted awake to the sound of music and a surprisingly tuneful accompanying baritone.

She shook herself, wondering how long she'd been sleeping, and, under cover of the music and Esquerez's singing, arranged herself more comfortably under the blanket. It had grown dark outside and, judging by the potholed state of the road that had the big car bumping and rattling like a toy, they had long ago left the principal highway behind.

She hugged herself secretly. Her plan was working. By now, they must be well on their way to Cabayan!

At that moment, the singing, which she was really rather enjoying, suddenly and abruptly ceased. The cassette was switched off and she could sense an air of concentration coming from the driver's seat. He hummed quietly to himself as the ground grew rougher, the big car lurching from side to side before being swung round to a sudden decisive halt.

She heard the handbrake creak, the engine switch off, then a click as the driver's door swung open.

And, all at once, her heart was beating wildly as she heard him come round to the back of the car. This was the inevitable moment she had been dreading. The time had come to account for her sins.

Her fingers were nervously clutching the blanket as she slid it down around her shoulders and waited anxiously, facing the door. Her little game was finally over. There was no point in trying to hide any more.

But, all the same, her heart turned over as she heard a key turn in the rear door lock and every prayer she had ever memorised seemed to spring soundlessly to her lips. Merciful heaven, let him not be too furious!

The door swung open and Kate's eyes squeezed shut as the beam of a torch shone in her face. Then she heard a growl, like that of some ferocious animal, followed by a spluttered, 'What the hell?' Then a strong hand was reaching in to grab hold of her and she was being hauled unceremoniously out into the open.

She half fell, half staggered to the ground, then was instantly, ruthlessly, snapped upright again. Esquerez gripped her arm with fingers of steel, as he shone the torch full in her face once more, shook her furiously and demanded, 'What the devil kind of game are you playing? Is this your perverted idea of a joke?'

In the harsh, reflected light of the torch his face was filled with a diabolical fury. The dark jaw thrust at her, hard and menacing, and the eyes like twin black lasers of malice seemed to enter her soul and rip it apart. If ever a man had murder on his mind, that man was standing right before her!

She frowned up into his face, searching for signs that he was bluffing, and, seeing none, resorted to defensive indignation. 'I had no choice! What else could I do? You refused to take me with you!'

'Precisely, *señorita*. I refused. And perhaps you would have been wiser to accept my refusal!'

At the tone of his voice, like roughly crushed razor blades, that seemed to scrape at her nerve-ends, making her shudder, Kate was suddenly acutely conscious that she was alone in the depths of the Philippine jungle at the mercy of a man she scarcely knew.

For one of the few times in her life she was filled with fear. Anxious to appease him, she found herself burbling, 'I didn't mean to make you angry. I thought you'd understand once I explained.'

'Did you, now?' His tone was sarcastic. 'Perhaps you even expected I might be pleased to see you? Well, I'm sorry to disappoint you, *señorita*, but at this moment the one thing that would please me most would be to wring your presumptuous little neck!'

He meant it, too. She could see that in his eyes, eyes that continued to burn down furiously at her. Kate's heart lurched within her. 'Don't you dare lay a hand on me! I'll fight you—and I'm stronger than I look!'

He threw her a look of unsmiling amusement. 'Is that a fact?' The black eyes flashed at her. Then, roughly, he stepped back, releasing his hold on her. 'In that case, I need have no compunction about leaving you to fend for yourself.'

'You wouldn't do that!' That prospect was appalling. Kate had to stop herself from reaching out to grab hold of him. 'How could I survive alone in the middle of the jungle? We're miles from anywhere, and there are wild beasts and things!'

'Indeed there are.' His tone was merciless. 'You should have thought of that before you hid in the car.'

'But I had to come with you!' Kate's tone was pleading. 'I promise you I didn't mean any harm by it. I really didn't think you would mind so much.'

'I suggest you didn't think at all, *señorita.*' All at once he had taken a step towards her. His hands were on his hips, his head flung back. He looked down at her with the eyes of a demon. 'How do you even know you can trust me? Are you in the habit of going off alone with men you barely know?'

Kate flushed, then felt the blood drain from her face. She shook her head stiffly. 'No,' she replied. 'But I didn't expect you would be alone. I expected you to stop off and pick up a guide.'

'A sort of chaperon?' He smiled. 'Someone to protect you from me should the need arise?' He let his eyes rove pointedly around the deserted clearing. 'Well, you have no chaperon, *señorita.* What do you propose to do about it?'

Kate swallowed and forced herself to hold his gaze. 'I propose to rely on your innate sense of chivalry. You have been at pains to assure me of your noble lineage. I shall simply expect you to behave accordingly—in a decent and civilised manner.'

The wide bow-shaped lips curved into a smile. Esquerez paused for a moment to look her up and down. 'You are rash, *señorita*, but you are also clever. You know how to appeal to a man's nobler impulses.'

Kate smiled shakily. Her appeal to his vanity had evidently done the trick. But his next remarks were destined to shatter her composure.

'However, *señorita*, I fear you ask too much.' Suddenly his smile had vanished. 'This is the jungle, and the jungle is not civilised. Here the strongest and the fittest, not the most decent, survive. I have already told you that my rules are not your rules. And the jungle has its own rules. They are harsh and cruel.'

Kate looked into his face, which was as harsh as the jungle. 'Are you trying to frighten me?' she challenged.

'Not to frighten you, to warn you.'

'That's very kind of you.'

'I do not mean to be kind. I intend only to caution you.'

Kate's heart, which had been beating like a tom-tom, was beginning to slow to a more normal rate. She looked into his face, at once noble and savage, and she was suddenly quite certain, in spite of his scowl, that she had nothing to fear from Vittorio de Esquerez. He might try to scare her with rough gestures and rough words, but he would never do her harm.

And besides, though she had learned nothing but bad about him from her fellow-journalists, in Hong Kong, apparently not even his very worst enemies had branded him a homicidal maniac.

She regarded him boldly. 'I think I can trust you. We may be in the middle of the jungle, but I do not think you are the type to behave like a wild animal.'

It was out before she realised the *double entendre*. She cringed at her blunder as, with a wolfish smile, Esquerez reached out to touch her hair. 'You do not think so, *señorita*? On the contrary, if it is your wish, I would be most willing to behave like a wild animal.'

In spite of herself, the touch of his hand was sending crackles of electricity over her scalp. Kate drew back from him sharply and regarded him sternly. 'My only wish is that we behave like two civilised people and try to make the best of the situation. After all,' she put to him, 'what's done is done.'

He dropped his hand away and continued to regard her, the humour dying in his eyes. And there was steel once more in his tone as he told her, 'What's done may be done, as you say, *señorita*. But it can also be *un*done. Take my word for it.'

Was that another of his threats? Kate looked back at him with defiant green eyes. 'And how do you propose to do that?' she put to him. 'Do you plan to drive me all the way back to Manila?'

'As a matter of fact, I don't.' He smiled at her grimly. 'But as surely as I'm standing here, there's no way you'll be continuing on to Cabayan with me!'

The panic stirred briefly inside her again, but she covered it with a show of bravado. 'So, what do you intend to do with me? Tie me to a tree and leave me here?'

Esquerez smiled grimly. 'Don't give me ideas.' His breath hissed with annoyance between his teeth. 'However, the solution I have in mind, though a little less colourful, will serve my purposes just as well. I have a friend who is based at a little coastal village about a day's drive away here. For us to get there will require a small diversion . . .' He paused and smiled an ironical little smile. 'But in the circumstances I shall be happy to make that sacrifice so that I may deposit you safely with him and make arrangements for him to accompany you back to Manila.'

Kate's heart sank within her. So near and yet so far! 'But why?' she protested. 'Since we've come this far, surely you may as well take me all the way?'

His face was set firm as he turned away and lifted the tent from the back of the car. Then, with a gesture of impatience, he flung it to the ground. 'Never! I warned you from the very beginning that I would never take you with me to Cabayan!'

'But *why*?' she insisted, her own frustration mounting. 'I told you I would be no trouble! Why won't you take me?'

'You're already trouble!' he snarled back at her. 'And I don't have to give you reasons!' He turned away abruptly, snatching the tent from the ground, and started to stride across the rough ground, away from her.

Suddenly, Kate was plunged into darkness. He had taken the torch and the only illumination that remained to separate her from the inky black night was the thin rosy glow from the rear lights of the Nissan. And all at once she was uncomfortably conscious of the depth of the silence that surrounded her.

They were in a small clearing, surrounded by trees so dense and so tall that they blocked out the moonlight. And who knew what manner of danger lurked around her? Some evil creature might spring out at any moment and drag her off into the steamy dark undergrowth.

Fear shuddered through her, jostling with her pride that was urging her to stay where she was and ignore him. Then, somewhere in the darkness, she heard a twig snap and, in an instant, her pride was conquered. On shaky legs she hurried after him.

As she came alongside him, Esquerez had dropped down on his haunches and was swiftly and expertly unrolling the tent. Without bothering to glance at her, he held out the torch. 'Hold this for me,' he commanded. 'Make yourself useful.'

Kate did as she was told, directing the beam where he was working, observing the sure, nimble movements of his hands and feeling her fear dissolve at his reassuring nearness. 'Is that a tent you're putting up?' she asked unnecessarily, really just to fill the silence.

As he began to slot the pieces of the steel frame together, he glanced up at her with impatient black eyes. 'It's not *a* tent, it's *my* tent,' he informed her sharply. 'I presume you brought your own with you?'

Of course, he knew she hadn't—his words were meant to chastise her and Kate lowered her eyes, accepting his chastisement. As a journalist who had travelled all over the world, she was well aware of the absolute necessity of equipping oneself with the tools of survival. And she had brought nothing with her, apart from a shoulder bag that contained a hairbrush, some pesos and a notepad and pencil, scarcely a survival pack for the jungle!

'I wasn't expecting to end up here,' she protested half-heartedly, feeling inept and foolish and, above all, unprofessional. 'I went to the Yacht Club expecting just to talk to you. Hiding in your car was a spur-of-the-moment thing.'

He appeared singularly unimpressed by her shame-faced disavowal. 'And I wasn't expecting to have company,' he told her, tossing the unfurled tent neatly over the frame. 'This tent, I'm afraid, is only big enough for one.'

'And where am I supposed to sleep? Out in the open, under a tree?'

'If you have a taste for sharing your bed with the local wildlife, that's entirely up to you.' He glanced at her maliciously and had the gall to smile. 'However, in your position, personally, I'd prefer the car.'

On rapid reflection Kate was inclined to agree. The local wildlife, she tended to suspect, would most likely be of the crawling, multi-legged variety. And though the back of the Nissan would not be the most comfortable of beds, it would at least be preferable to that.

She watched as he put the finishing touches to the tent, knocking in the pegs with a wooden mallet. 'OK, I'll sleep in the car,' she agreed.

'Wise choice, *señorita*.' He had finished with the tent and, brusquely snatching the torch from her hand, was striding back towards the car.

Indignantly, Kate followed him, her green eyes glaring. For a gentleman, sometimes he had damned few manners! Then she stood by and watched as he reached into the car and lifted out a plastic water bottle from one of the cardboard boxes. Her parched mouth aching—water, what a luxury!—she followed his movements with wide, pleading eyes as he raised the bottle to his lips and helped himself to a long, slow swig. Hurry! she urged him silently. Let me have my turn!

But as he finished drinking, pausing for a moment to wipe his mouth with the back of his hand, she felt a sharp flutter, almost of panic, as he calmly proceeded to return the water bottle to the box in the back of the car.

She took a step forward. 'What about me?'

Esquerez turned to look at her. 'What about you?' A look of callous incomprehension shadowed his face. 'As a professional anthropologist, with experience of such expeditions, I presume you at least brought your own supplies of food and water? I only brought enough for one.'

Kate felt a double pang of panic. It had almost slipped her mind that she was supposed to be an anthropologist! But more important than playing that part for the moment was her real and urgent need for water.

She glared at him now. 'You know damned well I didn't bring anything with me! I've already admitted that to you! And I need to drink! I'm dehydrated!'

'You should have thought of that before you stowed away.' He looked into her eyes without a glimmer of compassion. Then, just as she was starting to wonder if she might have to fight him for the water, he shook his head wearily and reached into the box again. 'So much for your assurance that you would be no trouble. You, *señorita*, are trouble to your fingertips!'

He lifted out the water bottle, but, as she tried to snatch it, he deliberately held it out of her reach. 'First things first.' He reached into the car again and drew out what looked like a packet of pills. He handed it to her. 'Salt tablets,' he told her. 'Take a couple with the water. Heaven knows how much salt you must have lost in perspiration while you were waiting for me in the car park.'

So, he was not, irretrievably, a sadist. He might even possess a grain of human compassion. Though as Kate took the tablets and drank back the water— like vintage wine to her parched mouth and throat— she seriously doubted that he had been motivated by compassion. More likely he simply wished to save himself the embarrassment of turning up at his friend's house with a corpse!

He was gathering up his sleeping-bag. 'I suggest we bed down right away. I want to get started early tomorrow morning, before it gets too hot.' Then he caught her eye. 'If you're hungry, there are some biscuits in that box. Personally, I don't want any. I had a pretty big lunch.'

Such generosity! But Kate shook her head. 'I'm not hungry either,' she told him. 'Just tired.'

'In that case, I'll say goodnight.'

As he started to move away, Kate nodded. 'Goodni——' But that was as far as she got.

There was a rustle in the undergrowth directly behind them, followed by what sounded like a cough. Kate stiffened abruptly, leaping sideways in alarm, and very nearly dropped the water bottle to the ground. 'What was that?' she croaked, her eyes darting around her. 'There's something behind us in those trees!'

With a faint smile Esquerez retrieved the water bottle and securely screwed its top back on. He looked down into her suddenly ashen face and assured her with amusement in his voice, 'There are many things in those trees, *señorita*. Many things we cannot see. But, don't worry, most of them are perfectly harmless. What you heard was probably just a bird or something.'

In spite of all the water she'd just drunk, the roof of Kate's mouth was suddenly bone dry. Probably just a bird, she repeated to herself. But it was the ominous 'or something' that filled her brain. And suddenly the thought of sleeping alone in the car paralysed her with a nameless dread. Surrounded by all those unfamiliar noises she would certainly be dead from cardiac failure long before the light of dawn!

She glanced up at Esquerez through lowered lids. 'Can't you make room for me in the tent?'

He raised one dark eyebrow. 'You wish to sleep with me? Now that is a development I had not expected so soon.'

Kate met his mocking gaze with emerald-hard eyes. 'Not sleep with you, Señor de Esquerez. Let's be perfectly clear about that. All I am asking is to share your tent.' She slid a nervous glance at the car. 'I don't really fancy sleeping on my own.'

For a long moment he looked down at her, saying nothing, and she could tell that some vigorous private debate was being conducted in his head. Then, by way of an answer, he reached into the car, snatched out the travelling rug and slung it over his shoulder, before quickly slamming the rear door shut and striding round to the front to switch off the lights.

'Vamos!' Then, without a glance in her direction, he was leading her through the darkness to the tent.

He lifted the tent flap and threw in the sleeping bag. 'You can have this,' he told her curtly. 'My honour as a gentleman demands this small sacrifice.'

His honour as a gentleman apparently also demanded that he did her the favour of undressing outside. Kate smiled to herself as she tussled with her rumpled trousers, then manoeuvred herself speedily into the soft, cool sleeping bag. Thank heavens for honour! she was thinking wryly.

By the time she heard him climb through the tent flap, then arrange himself in the blanket just inches away from her, her back was turned firmly in his direction, and her eyes shut tightly, feigning sleep.

As he bade her goodnight, she grunted in response, then in a flash of inspiration she half turned her head. It might be wise, she was thinking, to apprise him of the fact that she had seen him with the dark-haired girl at the Yacht Club and had easily guessed at the nature of their relationship. In the middle of the night, should his sense of honour suddenly find itself threatened by uncontrollable carnal urges, such a reminder would help to keep them in check!

Her tone carefully neutral, she observed, 'I hope your girlfriend wouldn't object to this arrangement. You can tell her when you see her that it was all perfectly innocent.'

She felt him smile in the darkness. 'The night is yet young. Reserve your judgement of innocence until the morning.' Then, as she turned irritably away from him and snuggled deeper into her sleeping bag, he bade her in that amused tone, 'Now go to sleep. Don't worry, I'll wake you if there's anything I need.'

But, in fact, he was asleep long before Kate. She could hear his peaceful, rhythmic breathing, while she stared, wide-eyed, into the night, wishing her own brain could switch off so easily.

But every aching nerve-end in her body was painfully, burningly, aware of his nearness and, in spite of herself, that nearness stirred her. Perhaps the sharing of the tent had not been such a good idea! Whether here with him or alone in the car, she seemed destined for a sleepless night.

But her body was exhausted and, in spite of the distractions, sleep began to pull her under. She was just drifting off when all of a sudden there was a thud and a crackle right behind her.

In a flash she was sitting upright, her body tense and rigid, as she clutched the sleeping bag to her trembling bosom and let out a strangled cry of fear. She reached out for Esquerez and gripped him by the shoulder. 'There's something out there, Vittorio! I heard it!' she squeaked.

Vittorio turned over with a sigh and urged her gently back on to the floor. 'It's nothing, *querida*,' he murmured softly. 'Just ignore it and go back to sleep.'

Then he was pulling the sleeping bag over her shoulders and drawing her tense body more closely against him, so that her spine curved comfortably against his chest and stomach, and the backs of her legs pressed warmly against his.

Kate made no effort to fight against him and, in spite of herself, she began to relax, finding the strong, firm pressure of the arm that embraced her warm and reassuring through the thickness of the sleeping bag.

'Sleep, *querida*,' he whispered softly, his breath a warm murmur against her hair. 'I'm here with you. You're perfectly safe.'

'Yes,' Kate murmured back in response, her body instinctively snuggling closer, all her fear miraculously evaporated, a dreamy contentment washing over her.

And a moment later, she was fast asleep.

Kate awoke next morning feeling rested and restored—and both disappointed and relieved to discover that Vittorio was already up, leaving her alone in the tent.

She flushed a little as she remembered the closeness they had shared last night, for she had slept like a baby in his arms till dawn. And, although she knew it should have felt wrong, it had felt like the most natural thing in the world.

Brusquely, she pushed the thought away, as she struggled once more into her crumpled beige trousers and ran her fingers through her tousled gold hair. It had felt natural because she'd been scared half to death—and, however despicable he might be, there was no denying that Vittorio de

Esquerez was that rare and particular breed of man with whom a woman instinctively felt safe. It was quite impossible to imagine even the direst of evils ever getting the better of him.

She smoothed out the creases in her cream cotton blouse and slipped her feet into her flat leather sandals, suddenly wishing that, survival pack aside, she'd had the foresight to equip herself on a more personal level for this crazy, hare-brained adventure. All she had with her were the contents of her shoulder bag—not even a toothbrush or a change of underwear, let alone a fresh pair of trousers and top! Before she even started the day, she was feeling decidedly uncomfortable and grubby.

She felt doubly so as she pulled back the tent flap and instantly caught sight of Vittorio. Looking irksomely fresh in a pair of faded blue jeans—not the light-coloured trousers he had worn yesterday—he was seated close by, in the shade of a tree, bent over the contents of a small tin frying pan that bubbled over a tiny calor gas stove.

As she stepped out of the tent, he glanced up to look at her, making her heart turn over most peculiarly.

'Good morning,' he bade her, a smile in the dark eyes. 'I trust you had an agreeable night?'

Kate met his smile with an inscrutable look. 'I slept quite well, if that's what you mean.'

'What else would I be meaning, *señorita*?' He held his eyes for a wicked moment, then deliberately resumed his stirring. 'I'm cooking us breakfast, as you can see. No doubt your restful night has restored your appetite?'

He was right about that. Kate nodded. 'I'm starving.' And she took a step closer to peer curiously into the frying pan. Whatever it was, it smelled delicious. Already, her mouth was starting to water.

'It's a local dish. Dried fish and rice,' Vittorio informed her without looking up. Then he picked up the pan lid that was lying close by and placed it firmly over the concoction. 'It'll be ready in about twenty minutes. Just time for you take a quick shower.'

He stood up and lifted the bucket of water that was propped against the side of the tree. 'I'll give you a tin mug that you can use to sluice the water over yourself.'

It was almost as though he had read her mind. The prospect of a good wash-down was like a promise of heaven. But this makeshift arrangement he was suggesting didn't appeal to her in the slightest. Kate's eyes narrowed argumentatively. 'You call that a shower? Surely there's a better way than that!'

Vittorio shrugged. 'What's the matter? Are you afraid I might watch you? Don't worry, your modesty is in no danger from me.'

But fears for her modesty were only a part of her reservations. Kate regarded him narrowly and hazarded a guess. 'I'll bet you didn't get washed with a tin mug and a bucket!'

He raised one dark eyebrow and paused for a moment, folding muscular arms over his deeply tanned chest. 'As a matter of fact, I didn't,' he conceded. 'There's a freshwater pool behind the trees. I had a dip in that.'

'Then I shall do the same!' Kate was indignant. 'Why didn't you just tell me about the pool right away?'

'Because I think it would be better if you took my advice and had a quick sluice down with the bucket and mug.'

'And why on earth should I do that? What's good enough for you is good enough for me!' Straightening her shoulders she began to march past him in the direction he had indicated—and found her way barred by an outstretched arm as firm and restraining as an iron bar.

'I advise against it, *señorita*.'

'Why?' She glared at him as he blocked her progress. 'Tell me why! I want to know!'

He looked down at her with those vivid dark eyes. 'Why not just do as you're told for once? You ask too many questions, *señorita*,' he chided.

His nearness and the touch of his arm against her breast was causing her breath to catch in her throat, but, with an effort, Kate answered in a calm, defiant tone, 'And, what's more, Señor de Esquerez, I'm used to getting answers! So, unless you can give me a very good reason why I shouldn't go and bathe in the pool, I'm afraid that's exactly what I'm going to do!'

For a moment their eyes locked, the green and the black, then in a gesture of impatience Vittorio dropped his arms. 'Do as you please,' he told her coldly. Then he turned abruptly and walked away.

'I damned well will do *exactly* as I please!' Kate muttered mutinously to herself, as she stomped off angrily between the trees. Who the devil did he think he was, trying to dictate to her like that?

Maybe, because she had been a little nervous last night, he had got it into his head that he could treat her like a child!

Well, he was wrong! She was an independent and capable young woman, perfectly able to look after herself!

The pool, she discovered, was less than twenty metres away, an inviting circle of cool green water overhung by lush green bushes and the pale trailing tendrils of eucalyptus trees. She kicked off her sandals and stuck in a toe. It was cool and delicious. She couldn't wait to get in.

She pulled off her blouse and rinsed it out quickly, then slipped off her trousers and did the same with these. They would dry in a trice in the warmth of the sun and they definitely needed freshening up.

Carefully, she draped them over the branch of a tree, then glanced round quickly to make quite sure that Vittorio hadn't secretly followed her before cautiously slipping off her bra and briefs and following exactly the same procedure with those. Then, with a smile of anticipation, she stepped into the water.

The water closed around her like a dream, making her sigh with pleasure as she sank back into its coolness, feeling her skin tingle and her scalp prickle deliciously as her hair spread out round her head like a fan.

Lazily, she swam a few strokes, loving the sensuous swirl of the eddies as they curled and moved against her naked body. Then she stretched her limbs and floated on her back, gazing up beyond the dense, soaring trees at the sky that hung over her like a shimmering blue canopy.

This was living! she smiled to herself.

She stayed in the pool for a good fifteen minutes and would have stayed longer if she had dared. But he had warned her that breakfast was nearly ready and she had not the faintest shadow of desire to provoke him into coming to look for her! As she started to climb out, a quick check reassured her that he was nowhere to be seen.

The water dripped like beads of crystal from her golden-skinned, slender, but generously curved body, with its full firm breasts, long legs and shapely hips, as she paused to shake back her shoulder-length hair and gently squeeze the water from it. Then, with a smile on her lips at the prospect of breakfast, she reached out to lift her clothes down from the tree.

But her blood all at once was like ice in her veins and her stomach turned into a block of cement, as she found herself looking into a pair of yellow eyes more evil than anything she had ever before witnessed.

'Merciful heaven!' was all she managed to whisper as raw fear gripped her and fixed her to the spot.

The evil eyes stared unblinkingly back at her. The cold and merciless eyes of a snake.

CHAPTER FOUR

IT WAS as though her body had turned to stone. Every fibre of Kate's being was gripped by paralysis as she stared aghast at the loathsome creature whose body was twined round the branch of the tree.

This must be a nightmare, she tried telling herself, but she knew it was sickeningly, horrendously real.

The snake's satanic yellow eyes stared balefully, threateningly, into hers, as its scaly dark head reared up a little and its tongue flicked from between its venomous jaws. And in a flash Kate knew for certain that at any second it would strike.

I shall die, she thought, as terror tore through her. Dear God, have mercy on my soul!

But at the very moment of abandoning hope, as she squeezed her eyes shut and waited for the moment that would send her soul to immortality, there was a sudden movement and a sharp singing sound, like the noise of cold steel slashing through the air. Then a dull thud as the decapitated body of the snake fell lifeless to the jungle floor.

A voice—the voice of some angel? she wondered—told her, 'It's all over, Kate. You're safe now.'

She blinked her eyes open as a strong hand grabbed hold of her and pulled her shivering body away from the tree. Then she was being drawn, in a dazed semi-stupor, into the embracing sanctuary of a pair of strong arms. Soft lips grazed her forehead, affectionate and reassuring, and suddenly she could no longer control the tears of relief that welled up painfully at the back of her eyes.

As a deep voice murmured, '*Dulce* Katharine. You're quite safe now. There's no more to fear,' the tears began to flow quite uncontrollably, her body racked by a painful sobbing that threatened to tear her poor heart in two.

'You saved my life,' she burbled incoherently, clinging to him and burying her face against his chest. 'If it weren't for you, that thing would have killed me. Right this minute I'd be dead.' She raised blurred eyes to look into his face. 'It *was* poisonous, wasn't it?' she asked, her voice trembling.

'King cobras usually are.' Vittorio smiled down at her grimly. Then as she shuddered in horror at the danger she'd been in, he kissed her temple and stroked her hair. 'Calm down, *querida*. It can't hurt you now.' Then his fingers came round to tilt her chin upwards, forcing her to look into his eyes, and the fine lips curved into a gently humorous smile. 'Surely you knew that I would save you? How could I possibly allow any harm to come to my charge?'

Through her tears Kate managed a wobbly smile. 'You must have been watching me all the time,' she accused him lightly, suddenly understanding in a flash why he had been so reluctant to let her bathe in the pool. 'Why didn't you just tell me there were snakes about?'

'And scare you to death? I didn't want to do that. You're already nervous enough of this place.' With his fingers he brushed her tears away, then bent to kiss softly the place where they had been. 'It's not just here at the pool that you can encounter snakes. You could walk into one almost anywhere.'

As her body tensed nervously at this revelation, Vittorio soothingly stroked her shoulders. 'Don't worry, *querida*. You're safe with me. I promise I won't let anything harm you.' Then, as the hand at her back seemed to draw her a little closer, Kate allowed her body to sink against him, feeling a shiver of something that was no longer fear sweep warmly, erotically, over her senses.

The warmth of him and the sweet clean tang of him in her nostrils was almost overpoweringly delicious. As his hand swept down her back to draw her more possessively against him, a secret sigh of surrender shivered through her. And her lips were parted and ready for his kiss as his mouth came down to cover hers.

It was a kiss whose subtle, erotic magic literally took her breath away. His lips were soft, yet wickedly masterful, igniting her senses with a lustful longing, as they teased and tantalised her own. And his tongue, as it flicked against the back of her teeth, sending charges of sheer carnality through her, was like an instrument of perfect torture, promising pleasures of which she had never dared dream.

'Oh, *querida*,' he murmured huskily, his body pressing hungrily, trembling against her.

And as his hand swept round to cup her breast, she heard herself breathe, 'Vittorio!' in response.

Her immediate temptation, the one she almost gave in to, was to press abandonedly against him. The hand that moulded her sensitive flesh, slowly circling, making her shiver, as his fingers grazed the taut, rosy nipple, felt strangely as though it belonged where it was. The delicious, sweet pleasure of this intimacy seemed like a part of her being that, until now, had been missing.

But in the very instant that she longed to succumb, horror-stricken sanity was moving in to save her. Had all sense of decency and propriety deserted her? Was she aware that she was standing, as naked as a hen's egg, in the arms of a man she scarcely knew?

Feeling hot colour flood through her from scalp to toe, she snatched her mouth from his and protested, 'Don't! Please don't! I don't know what came over me.' Then as his grip on her loosened, she hovered uncertainly, embarrassed to expose herself by stepping away. This, after all, was the very first time that she had ever been naked with a man.

He smiled and looked down at her, understanding. 'It's a little late now for modesty,' he observed humorously. 'I've already seen all there is to see.'

Feeling foolish, Kate felt her blushes deepen. Then, as she made to slip away from him and make a grab for her clothes, his grip around her tightened, holding her firm. 'I don't think it would be wise for you to go over there. Stay where you are. I'll get your things for you. I don't want you getting another scare.'

Of course. The snake. She nodded gratefully. 'I forgot,' she mumbled, as he released her. And she averted her eyes as he strode to the tree and lifted down her things from its branches. Dead or alive, she had no desire to set eyes on that loathsome creature again!

Vittorio pushed the pile of warm dry clothes unceremoniously into her arms. 'Get dressed, quickly,' he commanded. 'I want to have breakfast before it's totally spoiled!'

Kate clutched her things to her, to cover her nakedness, wondering how he could even *think* of eating after that ordeal. As he bent to pick up the long-bladed knife that he had used with such courage to slay the serpent and stuck it into the waist of his jeans, she shuddered and followed him nervously with her eyes.

'You'll stay close by?' she enquired, almost pleading. 'Don't go back to the tent until I'm ready.'

'I'll stay right here,' he promised her, grinning and leaning nonchalantly against a tree. 'Consider me your bodyguard and guardian angel. And for you, *señorita*, my services come free.'

Some angel! Kate was thinking, as she continued to clutch her clothes to her bosom. Her eyes swept the smoothly muscled shoulders and the strong arms with their sprinkling of fine black hairs that were folded now across his broad chest. Vittorio Esquerez was definitely all man, from the top of his handsome, sleek black head to the soles of his perfectly proportioned feet!

And, what was more, he was a man of a healthy, virile appetites, as he had already proved to her more than once. It would be an arrant and risky folly on her part, to mistake him, even superficially, for an angel!

She straightened her shoulders and informed him curtly, 'I'd just as soon you waited *behind* the tree.

If you don't mind, I'd like just a little privacy.'
Fighting her blushes, she met his eyes, as the be-
ginnings of a smile curled round his lips, and informed him with a sharp Irish scowl, 'I know
you've seen it all before, but that's no reason why
you should see it all again!'

Vittorio shrugged. 'What a hard woman you are!'
Then, with that impudent smile still hovering round
his lips, he executed a mocking little bow and did
as she had bade and stepped behind the tree.

A couple of minutes later, now hurriedly dressed
in her clean but lamentably crumpled blouse and
trousers, Kate was following him back to the
clearing where their tent was pitched and their
breakfast still bubbling. As she arranged herself,
cross-legged, under a tree and watched him scoop
their breakfast on to tin plates, she was aware of
how relaxed was the atmosphere between them.
There was barely a trace of the barbed antagonism
that had previously been the hallmark of all their
encounters.

As he held out her plate to her, she took it,
smiling. 'This smells absolutely delicious,' she told
him. Quite calculatedly, she met his eyes. Perhaps
something could be gained from this softening of
the atmosphere.

Vittorio sat down opposite her and handed her
a spoon. *'Buen provecho!'* he commended her.

'Buen provecho!' Kate responded, curling her
tongue with a fair degree of competence around the
Spanish equivalent of *bon appetit!* Then, as she
savoured a mouthful, she nodded approvingly.
'This tastes even better than it looks!' She glanced
across at him as he poured them both water. 'I hope

your girlfriend appreciates how lucky she is having a man with so many talents?' She fixed him with an almost coquettish smile. 'It isn't every day one comes across a man who can pitch tents in the dark and kill snakes before breakfast and then, on top of all that, cook wonderfully as well!'

He responded to her smile, but ignored her reference to his girlfriend, just as he had done the previous night. 'Indeed,' he agreed. 'I have many rare talents.' Then the bow-shaped upper lip quirked wickedly as he added, 'But don't waste your compliments on me, *señorita*. Sweet as they are, they will not change my mind.' As the smile fell from her face, his own smile broadened. 'Just as soon as we have finished breakfast, we'll be setting out for Bagu Bayo, where I shall deposit you with my friends who will take you back to Manila.'

Kate could have kicked him—and herself! She might have known he would be immune to flattery! A man with the pride and the inflated ego of Vittorio Felipe Salvador de Esquerez wouldn't give a button for her opinion of him. He already had a high enough opinion of himself!

She regarded him irritably and demanded to know, 'But why? Why are you so adamant about not taking me to Cabayan? What possible inconvenience could I be to you?'

By way of a response, Vittorio laughed out loud, displaying those magnificent strong white teeth of his. 'What possible inconvenience, indeed! Do you think I enjoy playing nursemaid, *señorita*? Is that all you think I have to do with my time?'

'*Nursemaid?*' Kate felt deeply offended. 'I've never needed a nursemaid in my life!' she protested, hurt that he should take her for some swooning female who folded up at the very first whiff of danger. 'I'll have you know,' she informed him stoutly, her shapely chin jutting to emphasise her point, 'that among my colleagues back in London I happen to have a well-earned reputation for being particularly able to look after myself. I've been sent on assignments all over the world, from the Middle East to Central America. I can assure you my editor wouldn't have sent me, if he'd thought I was the type who needed a nursemaid!'

As she paused for breath, cold horror drove through her. How could she have been so reckless? In her anxiety to defend herself, she'd given herself away!

Kate could see him change before her eyes. The good-humoured companion of just a few moments ago now wore a scowl as black as thunder. His suave civility had dropped away from him, like a silk curtain slipping from its rod, and seated before her was that other savage Esquerez whose rough-edged anger could strike fear in her soul.

He ground at her, 'Your *editor*? Anthropologists do not have editors for bosses.'

Kate held her breath, her heart beating within her. What could she say? She shook her head.

'So!' With great violence he had thrown his plate down on the ground, scattering the remains of his breakfast over the grass. 'You are not an anthropologist, after all! You lied to me. You are a journalist!'

Kate nodded miserably. 'I didn't mean to lie. Originally, I intended telling you the truth.'

With an impatient gesture, Vittorio sprang to his feet. '*Señorita*, it would appear that you never mean to do anything! You didn't mean to stow away in my car! You didn't mean to lie about your profession! What else have you done that you didn't mean to do?'

On the face of it, it was a pretty poor record, yet it was a gross misrepresentation of what she really was. It wasn't like Kate to make excuses for her actions and, normally, lying just wasn't in her character. She felt ashamed and uncomfortable as she excused herself once more.

'I only told you that stuff about being an anthropologist because, if I told you I was a journalist, I knew you would refuse to help me.'

'I refused to help you anyway. You could have saved yourself the bother!'

'Then it doesn't really make much difference, does it? It's not as though I tricked you into acting against your principles.'

'Which is as well for you!' His eyes fulminated anger. '*Señorita*, if there's one thing I cannot stomach, it's a liar!

'I'm not a liar!'

'That's a good one!'

'I'm not! I only did it because I was desperate. I could lose my job if I don't get this story!'

'That's not my problem. I don't give a damn! Maybe you deserve to lose your job!'

'You heartless bastard!' Kate felt like weeping. Didn't he know that if she lost her job, her brother would be forced to abandon his studies and the dream of a lifetime that Kate had shared with him, that one day he would become a doctor, would finally and forever be shattered?

She shook herself helplessly. No, of course he didn't know, and she didn't plan to tell him. He wouldn't give a damn about that, either.

He was standing over her, his face a mask of anger. 'So, now that the truth is finally out, we may as well have the entire story. What's the name of the paper you work for? And what exactly is your mission here?'

On stiff legs Kate pulled herself to her feet. Crouched there cross-legged on the ground while he towered furiously over her, she was beginning to feel like the worm he took her for. Looking him straight in the eye, she drew herself up tall and informed him with as much dignity as she could muster, 'I work for an English magazine called *Deadline*. And I'm here to write a story on the tribe of Cabayan.'

'Is that so?' His tone was scathing. Then suddenly he smiled a mirthless smile. 'Poor old Ramos. He must have been rather disappointed. I'm sure he was hoping that one of the big boys, like *Time* or *Newsweek*, would be the first to break the story.'

Kate met his harsh gaze without flinching. That he should seek to belittle her hardly surprised her, still she felt moved to speak up in *Deadline*'s defence. 'I realise you may not have heard of us. We're little known outside the British Isles, but *Deadline*'s a serious and respected paper none the less.'

'Serious and respected!' He spat the words with condemnation. 'What a pity it doesn't employ serious and respect-worthy journalists, instead of devious young women who appear to know no other way than to cheat and lie in pursuit of their stories!' He turned away angrily, then paused to glare at her over his shoulder. 'I suppose you thought you were on your way down to Cabayan to grab yourself the scoop of a lifetime? Too bad!' His eyes burned like hot tongs into her. 'I shall now take even greater pleasure in overseeing your immediate return to Manila!'

It would have been futile to try to change his mind, so Kate, for the moment, did not even try. Yet, in spite of the fact that she had now been unmasked, she was a long way from resigning herself to his will. However determined he was to return her to Manila, she was equally determined to get her story.

For Liam's sake, she told herself fiercely, although she was aware of a new edge to her determination. Nothing would give her greater pleasure than to get the better of the detestable Vittorio de Esquerez!

The temperature was soaring as they set off down the road, well up into the eighties and humid with it. And although Vittorio had told her that their destination was less than fifty miles away, their progress was excruciatingly slow. The route they were following was little more than a track hacked out of the living jungle. Left to itself, Kate could well imagine, without the occasional passing vehicle to keep it open, it would soon be swallowed up again. As it was, one could feel, like a living physical presence, the voracious jungle pressing in.

She'd had no idea it would be like this, she acknowledged to herself, shivering a little. And to think that she had embarked on this journey without so much as a compass to her name! In spite of all his sins, thank heavens for Esquerez. As long as she was with him, at least she would be safe.

She stole a secret glance at him, full of reluctant admiration. He drove through the jungle with the easy confidence of one negotiating nothing more demanding than some city highway, never once stopping to consult a map, manoeuvring the big vehicle around rocks and potholes and the occasional fallen branch of a tree, as though he did this sort of thing every day of his life.

And perhaps he did. Kate squinted at him curiously, realising how very little she knew about the man. She regarded the dark profile, with its strong, straight nose, square, chiselled jaw and high, proud forehead. With that volatile temperament of his, emotional quicksilver, he was impossible to slot into any familiar pigeon-hole. He was like no other man she had ever encountered. A mass of contradictions. An impossible mystery.

Suddenly curious, she turned to him and broke the silence between them. 'I've told you why I want to get to Cabayan. I'm after a story for my paper. But what about you? What takes you there? Why are you so interested in the lost tribe?'

He slanted her a look that was openly hostile. 'Do you want to put that in your story, too? Am I being subjected to some kind of interview?'

'Not at all!' Kate defended herself instantly. 'It was really just casual conversation. I simply asked out of personal interest.'

'In my experience there's no such thing as personal interest in a journalist. A journalist is always after a story.'

What a hopeless, twisted cynic he was! Still, refusing to be beaten, Kate persisted. 'I thought your company was involved in grand-scale civil engineering? Building conference centres in Hong Kong and five-star hotels in Singapore. Why this unbusinesslike diversion?'

In that final sentence she had not quite succeeded in keeping the censure from her voice. How could she, when Ramos had already told her that his only interest in the tribe was in exploiting them for cheap labour and depriving them of their land?

As he turned to look at her, he made no effort to defend himself. 'You appear to know a lot about me,' he observed.

She met his eyes. 'It's my job to know. It's all a part of being a good journalist.'

'So, suddenly you're a good journalist. That's quite a turnaround. A few minutes ago you told me you were in danger of being sacked.'

'Not sacked. Demoted.'

'Demoted. I see. So, all you're really worried about is taking a pay cut?'

Let him sneer all he liked, Kate thought in cold fury, not even deigning to turn round to look at him. A pay cut might not sound so drastic, but it was when you had people you loved depending on you and you were already stretched to your financial limit.

She threw him a harsh look. 'Yes, I'm worried about a pay cut. I can't bear the thought of having to cut down on the champagne and caviare and being forced to to cancel my dress account at Yves Saint Laurent.'

Vittorio laughed at her sarcasm and turned to cast an eye over her crumpled chain-store shirt and trousers. 'Is that where you got the outfit you're wearing?'

'You should talk!' Kate eyed his faded T-shirt. 'You're not exactly a fashion plate yourself.'

'In my job I don't have to be.'

'That's just as well.' She threw him a shrewd look. 'What is your job, anyway?'

'I thought you just told me that yourself. I run a company that builds five-star hotels in Hong Kong and conference centres in Singapore.' The black eyes swivelled briefly in her direction. 'I also like to involve myself from time to time in the occasional unbusinesslike diversion, as you call them. Cabayan is not the first one.'

Kate knew to what he was referring. They had told her in Hong Kong. 'I take it you're talking about your short-lived involvement with that youth centre project in the slums of Manila?'

He turned again to glance at her. 'Who told you about that? Ramos? I can just imagine how he managed to twist that story.'

'It wasn't Ramos.' But Kate did not elaborate. It was no business of his to whom she'd spoken in Hong Kong. There was no need at all for him to know that she'd received her information from some local journalists. No doubt he would have something to say about that! All that mattered was what they'd told her—that he'd very hurriedly backed out of the project in question when it had become clear that no profit was likely to be made from it.

But that, for the moment, was another story. Right now it was his involvement in Cabayan that interested her. She regarded him squarely. 'Why do you hate Ramos?'

Vittorio did not favour her with a glance. 'Because he stands for everything that I stand against. But his days are numbered. I shall see to that.'

It was a typically arrogant response. 'But what could you possibly have against him? He seemed to me a most generous man who's making a valuable contribution both to science and to his country. How can you justify interfering with his work?'

Vittorio laughed harshly. 'You do me an injustice. I don't just plan to interfere with it, *querida*. I intend to put a stop to it, once and for all. That was what I was in his office to tell him—and it's also why I'm on my way to Cabayan now.'

He turned then to look at her, his eyes dark and malicious. 'What a pity you won't be around to see the fireworks. It would be something else for you to write about for that pathetic little rag of yours!'

To her own slight surprise, the dig hurt a little. Kate regarded him narrowly. 'Why do you hate journalists?'

He paused for a moment. 'I hate them for the harm they do. I hate them for the way they go digging after stories without the least regard for who they damage in the process.'

So, he thought she was one of those foot-in-the-door journalists who preyed on other people's misfortunes. She put him right instantly. 'You misjudge me. *Deadline* isn't some grubby scandal rag. It's a highly regarded current affairs magazine. The stories we publish don't harm anyone. In fact, on the contrary, they often do good.'

That was something she believed with a passion. Many of the stories she had been involved with had succeeded in bringing the plight of the unfortunate, who otherwise would have had no voice, to the attention of a thoughtful and caring public. And though she was not about to confide this fact to one as cynical and uncaring as Vittorio de Esquerez, the knowledge that it was so gave her enormous satisfaction.

'So, you're a regular little Samaritan, are you?' His response was as scathing as Kate had expected it would be. 'Please don't tell me any more. I don't think I could stand it. It's a little early in the day for hearts and violins.' Then, with a contemptuous gesture, he switched on the cassette player and proceeded to hum along to the Rodrigo concerto that suddenly blared out from the quadrophonic speakers.

The arrogance of the man! The utter rudeness! He, apparently, had had enough of their conversation and so, unilaterally, it was terminated!

Kate clenched her fists into balls to control the sudden impulse that tore through her to reach out and switch the cassette player off. She turned to him and shouted a little more loudly than was necessary, 'You don't like opposition, do you? You only like people who always agree with you. What makes you think you're so damned superior?'

He ignored her as though she had never spoken. He simply frowned a little, as though concentrating on his driving, and kept his eyes fixed on the road.

Kate began to bristle with indignation. If there was one thing she couldn't stand, it was being ignored. She raised her voice a couple of decibels. 'I was saying you don't like opposition, do you? You only like people who always agree with you!' Then, as he continued to hum and ignore her totally, her patience snapped and with a gasp of anger her hand reached out towards the offending cassette player.

But her fingers never reached the switch. With the lethal speed of a striking cobra Vittorio's hand had caught her by the wrist. His fingers dug mercilessly into her flesh. 'Are you looking for a fight?' he gritted.

Startled by the speed of his response, Kate found herself blinking into his face. 'Why would I be looking for a fight? All I did was ask you a question.'

'Is that what it was?' The black brows drew together. 'It sounded to me like someone picking a fight.'

He was right, of course, but she would be damned if she would admit it. Kate wrestled to free her arm from his grip and threw him a look of cold green fury. 'Are you trying to amputate my hand?' she spat at him. 'Or do you simply enjoy bullying defenceless women?'

'So, you're defenceless now?' Still he held her. 'I thought you told me you could look after yourself?'

'When I'm dealing with civilised people I can. I confess I'm not used to dealing with savages!'

'But you knew I was a savage. You should not have sought me out. Unless, of course...' His eyes raked her face. 'Unless you have a secret liking for savages.'

'Don't flatter yourself!' But she looked away. There had been something in his tone as he had made the accusation, just the faintest hint of sexual menace, and something in the way her blood had responded, leaping like a wild thing in her veins, that had caused her a sudden flash of discomfort.

'Don't flatter yourself!' she repeated with anger. 'If it wasn't that I need to get to Cabayan, I wouldn't have come within a million miles of you!'

'I'm glad to hear it.' He flung her hand aside, then with an angry gesture switched off the cassette player. 'It's a relief to know,' he told her coldly in the sudden silence that descended, 'that our mutual antipathy is all we have in common.'

Kate sat back in her seat and rubbed her wrist that still tingled where he had gripped it so tightly. At least he was right about one thing, she conceded. Their mutual antipathy *was* the only thing they shared.

But no way would she allow him to have the last word. Glaring straight ahead of her through the windscreen, she observed, her tone biting, 'By the way, there was no need for you to tell me the purpose of your visit to Cabayan. Ramos already told me what you're up to.'

He did not answer, and his silence was contemptuous. Again, Kate felt anger stir within her.

She slid him a glance and continued with venom, 'You're planning to exploit these poor tribespeople. All you care about is making a profit out of them.'

She might have been an ant on the jungle floor for all the attention he was paying her. Kate felt her anger boil into indignation. She swung round to accuse him, her green eyes flashing. 'You're a real superior bastard, aren't you? Nothing and no one really matters to you—just so long as you're in control!'

The words had barely left her lips before the Nissan stopped with an excruciating judder as Vittorio jammed his foot down on the brake. Feeling the breath knocked out of her, Kate grabbed at the dashboard, half fearing she was about to shoot straight through the windscreen.

'What the devil was that all about?' Blinking dazedly, she looked around her, half expecting to see some ferocious wild animal inconveniently blocking their path. But the track ahead of them was empty. There appeared to be no good reason why he had stopped.

Without looking at her, Vittorio pushed open the driver's door and jumped down on to the dusty track. 'I feel like a break. Make us some coffee. The pots and things are in the back.'

All that was missing was a snap of his fingers. He had issued an order as though she were some minion. Hot, fierce anger went flooding through her. 'Are you talking to me?' Kate demanded through clenched teeth.

He turned then to look at her, a picture of male arrogance. 'Who would I be talking to? I see no one else here?'

'I thought perhaps you were talking to some servant. I'm not accustomed to being spoken to that way.'

A mocking dark smile flitted over his features. He came to lean casually against the car door. '*Señorita*, you are too sensitive. One in your position, who apparently thinks nothing of imposing her company on others, really has no right to expect privileged treatment. Besides,' he added, leaning a little closer, 'I seem to remember you offering me your services as a cook and general helper on the journey. All I'm doing is taking you up on that offer.'

Kate glared at him, hating him. 'You're absolutely right. I really have no right to expect any better treatment from a man as insensitive and as arrogant as yourself.'

He was still looking down at her, his dark eyes mocking. 'So, now that we both understand the situation... *Señorita*, kindly make the coffee.'

Kate scowled at him mutinously. Given the choice, she would sooner make him a cup of arsenic.

'Oh, by the way...' he had started to turn away, but paused now to fix her with another dark look '...what you were saying a moment ago... As it happens, you were perfectly right. I fully intend to exert total control—down in Cabayan or anywhere else that takes my fancy. Small fry like Ramos, and yourself, can squeal all you like, but you're wasting your time. Things will be done according to my plans and nobody else's!'

As he strode away, Kate was trembling with anger. The man's towering arrogance knew no bounds. But, if he had intended to intimidate her, he had failed utterly. This autocratic little display of his had simply made her even more determined to see her mission through to the end.

She glared at his back. By all the saints, she would find a way, if only just to spite him, to get to Cabayan and get her story! This time the great Vittorio de Esquerez had seriously underestimated his adversary.

She snorted defiantly as she reached for the coffee things. Before very long he would find that out!

CHAPTER FIVE

THEY arrived at Bagu Bayo, as Vittorio had predicted, just a couple of hours before nightfall.

One moment they had been bumping through the seemingly endless jungle, when all at once the vegetation dropped away and they were heading into a scrubby clearing dotted with neat wooden houses perched on stilts.

Kate felt herself perk up with anticipation. After the uncomfortable monotony of the jungle, with its dark, brooding silences and constant air of menace, this place, primitive as it appeared, was like a welcome breath of civilisation. Little knots of men, bare-chested or in T-shirts, and brightly dressed women with long, glossy hair were going about their business in leisurely fashion, while a group of laughing, barefoot children played with a puppy under a tree.

And, as the Nissan made its way between the houses, past a little wooden café and a grocery store, sending up clouds of dust into the air, people turned to smile and wave, as though welcoming to their midst a long-lost friend.

'They appear to know you,' Kate remarked grudgingly, wondering why they should be so pleased to see him. Perhaps, she decided, with a flash of cynicism, someone had paid them to put on this display.

Vittorio made a sudden turning which took them out of the clearing and on to a made-up road—and there before them, like some magical vision, stretched the shimmering sapphire of the sea.

A short drive later they were approaching a cluster of houses built in southern European style—with carefully tended gardens at the front and pretty verandas bright with potted flowers.

'We're here,' Vittorio informed her, swinging the big car through a pair of narrow iron gates and on to a pink-stoned, crazy-paved driveway. 'This is where Alfonso and Didi live. They're the ones who'll be taking you back to Manila.' Then, ignoring her scowl, he banged his fist on the horn, and, an instant later, a pretty Filipina came rushing through the front door and down the steps to greet them.

'Vittorio!' she squealed, throwing herself into his arms, as he stepped down from the Nissan and strode towards her. 'What a wonderful surprise! Why didn't you tell us you were coming?'

'You're looking great!' Vittorio embraced her warmly, making Kate smile secretly as she watched the scene. The girl, whom she guessed must be Didi, looked like a fragile doll in the tall Spaniard's arms, and it was evident that there existed much fondness between them.

It was somehow odd, and a little touching, to witness this perfectly spontaneous and affectionate exchange. For it was the very first time, Kate found herself observing, that she had seen him with his defences totally lowered. Even that time she had seen him with his girlfriend at the Yacht Club he had not been as free and relaxed as this.

Kate climbed down a little self-consciously from the Nissan and waited to be introduced.

As Didi caught sight of her, her expression changed. With a flash of bewilderment in her dark almond eyes, she blinked at Kate, then turned back to Vittorio. 'You've brought a friend with you,' she observed politely, quite clearly at a loss how to interpret the situation.

'More of an acquaintance, a very recent acquaintance.' Vittorio was quick to put her right. 'This is Miss Kate O'Shaughnessy,' he offered, as Didi came forward to shake Kate's hand. 'She's a journalist from London,' he elaborated coolly, 'and I'm afraid she's got a little lost. I was hoping you and Alfonso could do me the favour of escorting her back to Manila.'

'We'd be delighted!' Didi agreed. 'Alfonso's down at the power-station right now, but he should be back in about an hour.' She turned to address Kate with a look of concern. 'The Philippine jungle is far too dangerous a place for a woman on her own. You were very lucky to have bumped into Vittorio.'

'I was on my way to Cabayan,' Vittorio intervened before Kate could say a thing. 'I came upon her in the middle of the jungle, literally miles from anywhere.' He paused deliberately to catch Kate's eye, a smile of devilment sparkling in his own. 'I couldn't spare the time to take her back myself and I know you and Alfonso go up to Manila regularly. I knew you wouldn't mind taking on an extra passenger.'

'Of course not!' Didi exclaimed. 'As a matter of fact, we're planning to go up tomorrow. You really couldn't have timed it better!'

Kate gritted her teeth and tried to look grateful, as she abandoned the half-formed plan in her head. For it had been in her mind just a moment ago to play this scene very differently.

Perhaps, she had calculated, if she were to create a fuss and throw herself on the mercy of his friends, she might succeed in winning their support and persuade Vittorio to relent. But Didi had proved to be such a likeable person that, at the very last minute, she had revised her strategy and decided to fall in with Vittorio's story. Not for his sake, but for Didi's. She had no desire to create unpleasantness in the midst of such genuine warmth and harmony.

I shall just have to think of another way, she told herself dolefully as Didi proceeded to lead them indoors.

They were seated in the airy, spacious sitting-room, enjoying their second round of coffee and cakes and just chatting generally about this and that, when Vittorio suddenly enquired of Didi, 'So, how's the project going? No problems, I hope?'

Enthusiastically, Didi shook her head. 'Not a single problem, I'm happy to say. And the villagers are behind us all the way.' She cut a smiling glance across at Kate. 'You should have seen this place a year ago!'

Kate frowned in response. 'I'm sorry...' she began. She hadn't a clue what Didi was talking about.

'Didn't Vittorio tell you about the village?' Didi glanced at Vittorio, then back to Kate. Then, as Kate shook her head, she looked back at Vittorio. 'You shouldn't be so modest!' she chided. Then, as Vittorio shrugged and sat back in his chair, she turned to address herself to Kate once more.

'This village is one of Vittorio's special projects— there are scores more like it all over the Philippines. You see, many of these villages are so remote that they're virtually living in the dark ages—no electricity, no roads, no schools—and it's the project's aim to change all that. So far, here in Bagu Bayo, thanks to Esquerez Engineering, there's a new electricity power-station, a few miles of road and a brand new school. Six months from now there'll also be a hospital. As you can imagine, the place has been transformed. The people think the whole thing's a miracle.'

With a teasing laugh she turned her sloe eyes on Vittorio. 'And they think that you're a miracle worker!'

Feeling deeply perplexed, Kate followed the girl's gaze to the bronzed, impassive face of the man sitting opposite them. If what Didi had just told her really was true, and she could think of not a single reason to doubt it, it was all a very far cry indeed from the things she had been told by Ramos and the others!

Far from being an exploiter and profiteer, it appeared that in fact he was something very different—or at least that Kate had heard only part of the story. The man she had condemned as a total charlatan, on this new evidence, was a public benefactor!

As she wrestled uncomfortably with this revelation, Kate could feel her confusion and bewilderment growing. Why would anyone have bothered to invent such stories? The situation was growing curiouser by the minute!

Vittorio was shrugging off Didi's compliments. 'If you ask me, it's your husband who's the miracle worker. He's the one who runs the project. He's the one who keeps it going.'

As he spoke, he kept his gaze fixed studiously away from Kate, although she knew he was conscious of her eyes upon him. Suddenly, she was seeing him in a totally new light, a light which, she found herself acknowledging reluctantly, really rather suited him—or, at least, the intermittent, more noble side of him! Then, at the sudden sound of a car outside, Vittorio winked at Didi. 'Talk of the devil!'

Instantly, Didi jumped to her feet. 'You're right, it's Alfonso!' Her face was suddenly glowing. 'He's back a little early. He must have heard you were here!' Then she rushed to the door to embrace her husband, as a moment later a smiling man in a khaki drill suit came striding into the room.

He was shorter than Vittorio and more leanly built, but he had the same Spanish colouring, the same dark hair and eyes, though he lacked Vittorio's striking presence, that unique power to draw all eyes to himself.

And, exactly as she had for Didi, Kate felt a liking for Alfonso straight away. They were a charming and delightful couple, she decided, watching with a curious twinge of envy as they collapsed into a sofa, side by side. The sort of couple it was a pleasure just to be with.

Later, they had dinner, a sumptuous affair—with traditional roast pig and all manner of side dishes, and, for dessert, a selection of mouth-watering rice cakes wrapped up in banana leaves.

To Kate's relief, one subject was never mentioned—the subject of her imminent dispatch back to Manila. For the fact was she was really thoroughly enjoying being a part of this unlikely foursome. The thought of being summarily ejected was, in a curious way, depressing.

The conversation, however, was far from that. Kate listened with amusement to the masculine banter that was clearly a regular feature between Vittorio and Alfonso. Watching them together it was hard to believe that one was the head of a huge corporation, while the other was his employee, a comparatively lowly engineer. Clearly, above all considerations of status, the two were first and foremost friends.

'It was great when Vittorio was living with us, at the time when the power-station was begun,' Didi confided to her guest, as the two women prepared coffee in the kitchen. 'This is the third project Alfonso has been put in charge of. We'll be moving on to another one soon.'

Kate was making up some powdered milk in a jug. 'Don't you get lonely living in places like these?' she asked.

Didi shook her head emphatically. 'I could never get lonely as long as Alfonso's around, and I always try to involve myself in the life of the village. I run handicraft groups, things like that. I even take the occasional class at the school.

'Of course, sometimes, I do miss the city. That's why we go back to Manila for regular weekends. To keep in touch with family and friends and stock up with provisions you can't get here. Like fresh milk,' she laughed, taking the jug from Kate and setting it on the tray with the other coffee things. 'But it's surprising how easily one adapts. I know I'd miss life out in the villages if we had to move back to the city permanently.'

In a strange way Kate could appreciate that. Primitive and isolated as it was, Bagu Bayo was a fascinating little place. And, besides, she surmised with a strange twist inside, as she followed Didi back into the dining-room, it must in itself be immensely rewarding to be involved in these schemes that changed the lives of the villages. Didi's contentment with her lot was not really so surprising—especially when one considered the blessing of her marriage. For it was perfectly clear that she and Alfonso absolutely adored one another.

Throughout the entire course of the evening there was only one faintly jarring note, which really should not have been jarring at all. Yet Kate's coffee-cup hovered halfway to her lips as Alfonso suddenly enquired of Vittorio, 'So, tell us—how's Carmen keeping these days?'

The moment that ticked past before Vittorio gave his answer seemed to Kate to stretch into eternity. For she knew in an instant that Carmen was the girl whom she had seen with Vittorio at the Yacht Club. And for some strange reason it required quite an effort for her to take a mouthful of her coffee and lay her cup back on its saucer without spilling any.

'Carmen's fine. Busy as usual.' Vittorio was smiling as he replied.

'How's her new business going?' Didi wanted to know. 'Last time I spoke to her she was just getting established.'

'Oh, her business is thriving. But you know Carmen. Anything she takes on she makes a success of.' There was a note of pride in Vittorio's voice as he elaborated, 'And running this new fashion house of hers is work she's admirably suited to. Few people have more of a flair for fashion than Carmen.'

There was no earthly reason why this conversation should upset her, but to Kate's shock and astonishment, it did. It was simply that it had come as an unexpected digression, she told herself firmly, rationalising her feelings. Since she was the only one of the foursome who was unacquainted with Vittorio's girlfriend, suddenly she had felt like an outsider.

And an unkempt and dishevelled outsider at that! For, all at once, she was acutely conscious of her hopelessly crumpled shirt and trousers. Since she had rinsed them out in the pool this morning, they hadn't come within a mile of an iron!

She recalled how Vittorio had drawn attention to her state of dress in the course of their conversation in the car—and, in the very same instant, an electrifying image of the strikingly beautiful, sophisticated young woman whom she had glimpsed so briefly at the Yacht Club flashed almost tauntingly across her brain. A girl like that, she knew for certain, would never be seen dead in a state like this!

Didi was glancing across at her with a smile of apology. 'I don't suppose you know who we're talking about.' Then, with a teasing wink at Vittorio, she elaborated, 'Carmen is the future Mrs de Esquerez.'

The future Mrs de Esquerez? Kate felt her jaw drop. She blinked across at Vittorio, as though for confirmation.

He let his eyes slide away. 'We are expected to marry.' Then, clearly reluctant to pursue such a personal subject, he smiled across at Didi. 'This coffee is delicious.'

That was all that was said on the subject of Carmen. Throughout the evening her name was not mentioned again. And Kate very quickly recovered her equilibrium and put the matter out of her head. After all, what could it possibly matter to her that the girl was Vittorio's wife-to-be? There was not a single thing about the man that mattered to her personally.

She kept that thought determinedly in front of her for the remainder of the evening and took it with her when she climbed into bed. Yet, irritatingly, in spite of her tiredness, it took her considerably longer than usual to fall asleep.

All sorts of distractions were tumbling through her head. Didi's revelation about Vittorio the benefactor, the mystery of Ramos—and her own personal predicament. For she still hadn't figured out a way of persuading Vittorio to take her to Cabayan.

But it was none of these thoughts that stayed stubbornly with her until the moment when she finally drifted off. It was the thought and the image of a dark-haired beauty, whose introduction into the conversation earlier that evening had caused her such unexpected pain.

For, suddenly, one name and one face seemed to haunt her. She could think of only one thing.

Carmen.

Kate awoke next morning to the sounds of busy activity. Clearly, she was the only person in the house who was still in bed.

A trifle guiltily she stretched and yawned and snatched a quick glance at her watch. It was after seven-thirty, late for the tropics, where the day's activities invariably started early because of the impossible afternoon heat.

She threw back the thin sheet and jumped from the bed, praying that Vittorio had not already left. She still had no idea how she was going to do it—especially with so very little time left to do it in—but she was as determined as ever to persuade him to take her with him.

She pushed back the sleeves of Alfonso's pyjama jacket—all of Didi's nightdresses had been far too small for her!—then she crossed to the window and pushed open the shutters, leaned forward and peered outside.

How very strange! The sun wasn't shining! She frowned a little and peered up at the sky. This was almost like being in England! A thick blanket of clouds hung low in the sky.

Oh, well. She crossed to the chair where a pair of Alfonso's generously loaned trousers and one of his shirts were carefully draped. At least it was still warm, almost oppressively so. One couldn't expect the sun to shine every day!

The clothes fitted her not too badly—a little big and a little baggy, but with the aid of one of Alfonso's leather belts she managed to make herself look presentable. And it was a positive joy to be wearing something that was properly pressed for a change! Her disastrously crumpled blouse and trousers had been whisked away last night by Didi.

'I'll have them laundered and pressed for you before we leave for Manila,' she had thoughtfully promised her guest. Little did she realise that Manila was not the destination Kate had in mind!

After a quick wash Kate went through to the kitchen to find Didi by the cooker, her expression serious, though her frown momentarily vanished as she caught sight of Kate. 'How are you this morning? Did you sleep well?'

'Like a log,' Kate assured her gratefully. 'I'm sorry I slept a little late. I hope I haven't held you up?'

Didi shook her head. 'Oh, don't worry about that. It looks as though none of us will be going very far today.'

Kate blinked in surprise. 'Why on earth not? Has something happened?' she wanted to know.

'Not yet, but it's about to,' a deep voice informed her. 'Within a couple of hours, I'd say.'

As Vittorio came through the door behind her, Kate whirled round with a start to look at him. And

to her stupefied and intense irritation her heart flew
to her throat just at the sight of him.

He was dressed in jeans and a faded sleeveless
T-shirt, his feet thrust into a pair of rubber flip-
flops, and the dark-tanned chest and muscular
shoulders bore the sheen of strenuous physical
labour. He brushed the film of perspiration from
his brow with the back of one slightly grubby hand
and threw her a faintly rueful smile. 'I'm afraid
there's a typhoon on the way. It looks as if we're
stuck here until it's passed over.'

'A typhoon?' Kate repeated, barely taking his
words in, aware only of a sense of relief and elation
that she had just been granted a stay of execution.
Fate had generously given her a little more time to
work on some plan to win him over.

He was looking at her impassively with those
splendid black eyes. 'You do know what a typhoon
is, I presume?' he enquired.

'Of course I know!' He was making fun of her.
'Though I've never actually experienced one, I
confess.'

Vittorio had crossed to the kitchen sink and was
washing his hands vigorously under the tap. 'Well,
you're about to now. Something else for you to
write about.' He shot Kate a brief, lightly scathing
glance as Didi handed him a towel. 'Before the wind
gets up the sky will turn black. You may have noticed it's already pretty dark now?'

Kate nodded. 'Yes, I did. Though I'd no idea
what it meant.'

'Well, it's usually one of the first signs that a
typhoon is on its way. The next sign we'll have is
when the rain starts to fall—not too heavily at first,

but turning into a deluge as the wind gets up.' He finished drying his hands and laid the towel aside. Then he crossed to the fridge and took out a jug of water. 'And the wind will be ferocious. Be prepared for that. Like nothing you've ever experienced in your life.'

He nodded towards the palm trees in the garden outside. 'Right now they're standing the right way up, but when the typhoon strikes they'll be bent over double. And anything that isn't able to bend with the wind is in danger of being snapped in two or torn out by the roots. A typhoon has no mercy. It's an indiscriminate destroyer. That's why Alfonso and I have been up checking the roof and putting extra supports in the perimeter fencing.'

He paused and smiled at her frown of concern, as he poured some water into a tumbler and drank. 'Don't worry, this house is in no danger of being blown down. It's the houses of the villagers that are in most danger. Just make sure that your bedroom shutters are fastened, stay indoors and you'll be perfectly safe.'

'Can't I do anything to help?' Kate resented slightly being advised to stay indoors. 'Surely I could make myself useful?'

Vittorio returned the water jug to the fridge, then paused on his way to the outside door. 'Just stay indoors. I'll let you know if I find any use for an able-bodied female.' A flicker of amusement crossed his face as the dark eyes looked her up and down. 'By the way, that outfit suits you,' he observed, taking in the loose, doubled-up trousers and the voluminous white shirt that made her look unusually vulnerable.

Kate responded with a jokey smile. 'It's my Charlie Chaplin look,' she quipped. 'I've got the bowler hat and cane next door.'

Vittorio winked and held her eyes, responding warmly to her humour. 'I look forward to a full dress performance later.' Then he smiled once more and hurried outside.

The storm unfolded more or less as Vittorio had warned, each stage following upon the last with an eerie sense of inevitability.

Suddenly, the sky was as black as night and huge splots of rain began to fall. Then the wind from the sea, which had been but a breeze, began to stiffen to a howling gale. The splots of rain, in the blink of an eyelid, had united to form a driving sheet of water, and all at once the air was filled with the shrieking, blood-curdling, animal-like roar of the mercilessly descending typhoon.

Kate glanced at Didi as the shutters began to rattle, as though the storm was struggling to force its way inside. 'What about Alfonso and Vittorio?' she asked nervously. 'Isn't it time they came indoors?'

Didi pulled a face. 'If I know them, they won't come in until the storm is good and over.'

Kate's jaw dropped open. 'But it's dangerous out there! There must be all sorts of debris flying around!'

'I know, I know. Please don't remind me.' Didi's lovely almond eyes reflected her fear. 'But at times like this the villagers need all the help they can get, and Alfonso and Vittorio aren't the types to stand by.'

'But they might get killed!' That thought was appalling, but instantly Kate regretted expressing it out loud. She reached out a comforting hand to Didi and laid it on her slender arm. 'On the other hand, I'm sure they can take care of themselves. A couple of big, strapping men like them!'

Didi pursed her lips and lowered her eyes. 'Let's just pray to God that they can,' she sighed.

But prayers alone were not enough for Kate. As Didi comforted herself with cups of coffee, Kate prowled the house like a restless animal, her senses driven mad by the relentless baying of the wind all around them. What was happening out there? she wanted to know. It sounded like the end of the world.

It was just as she was feeling that she could bear it no longer that she heard a loud rattling coming from the bathroom. She pushed open the door and peered inside and saw at once that one of the shutters had been blown open. She hurried to the window to fix it, reaching outside to pull it to, but curiosity made her pause for a moment to examine the storm-torn scene outside.

To her amazement, there were people everywhere. Villagers—men and women and children—every one of them drenched to the skin, as they battled against the destruction all around them. A group of them were fighting to hold the battered fence in place, while beyond the fence, amongst the native houses, some built on stilts, some built on the ground, more courageous little groups were struggling to keep walls and roofs from blowing down.

Through the lash of the rain and the skirling wind Kate could hear them shouting encouragement to one another. And suddenly her brain was filled with one question: what on earth was she doing in here?

With sudden resolution she pulled the shutter closed and marched through to the sitting-room to Didi. 'I'm going out there to help,' she announced. Then, as Didi opened her mouth to protest, she was heading unstoppably for the door.

The force of the wind almost lifted her bodily from the ground, wrenching the air from her lungs and making her lurch drunkenly forward. And the lash of the rain was like a solid wall of water, soaking her from head to toe in seconds. But nothing in the world could have stopped Kate now, as she headed gamely for the nearest group of villagers.

As heads turned round curiously at her approach, she shouted in English, 'I'm here to help! Tell me what to do!'

It was doubtful if any one of them understood a single word, but at times of crisis the barriers of language fell away. Her purpose was written in her eyes and on her face and was greeted with instant, grateful smiles.

'Miss! Miss!' An old man instantly grabbed her attention, frenziedly waving his skinny brown arms in the direction of one of the flimsy native houses, where a woman with a small child clinging to her drenched skirt was fighting a losing battle to keep the walls intact.

Instantly, Kate was clambering through a hole in the fence, stumbling and staggering as she went.

'I'm coming!' she called out to the lone embattled woman. 'Hang on! I'm coming to give you a hand!'

After that, she was moving from house to house, without waiting to be asked, just going where she was needed, and she had totally lost all track of time when suddenly she was aware of a figure behind her grabbing her by the arm and swinging her round to face him.

'What the hell are you doing here? I thought I told you to stay indoors!'

Her was mud-spattered and dirty, much like herself, jeans clinging wetly to his thighs, the sleeveless T-shirt ragged and torn and plastered like a second skin to his chest. There was a smudge of dirt down one side of his jaw and the dark hair was hopelessly dishevelled. Yet as Kate looked up into the jet-black eyes it seemed she had never seen a sight more magnificent.

The feeling, evidently, was not reciprocated. Vittorio gave her another shake. 'Is Didi with you?' he demanded. 'Don't tell me you persuaded her to join you in this madness?'

Kate sought to jerk her arm away, with her free hand pushing her wet hair from her face. 'No, Didi isn't with me. She stayed in the house.' She met the accusing black eyes defiantly. 'But don't think you can send me back to join her! I'm staying here where there's work to do!'

'That's where you're wrong! But I'm not sending you, I'm *taking* you—back to the house this very minute!'

As he started to drag her over the mud, Kate slithered helplessly, unable to resist him. No matter how desperately hard she tried her feet just couldn't get a grip. Half staggering, half falling, she squealed in protest. 'Let me go! Let me go! You have no right to do this!'

Vittorio flung round to scowl at her. 'I have every right! While you're in this place, you're *my* responsibility!'

'I'm damned well not! I'm my *own* responsibility! I don't need anyone to take care of me!'

'It seems you do!' He was relentless. 'I've never in my life met anyone as reckless and pig-headed as you!'

It was at that moment that, in her struggling, Kate stumbled and fell, and, as she dropped to the ground, the sudden jerk caused Vittorio's wet hand to lose its grip on her. Sprawling in the mud, she glowered up at him.

'You don't want to take me back because you're worried about my safety! You're just angry because I didn't do what I was told! Why, for once, don't you stop trying to control everything and realise that I'm here to help and that my contribution is as vital as anyone else's?' She looked deep into his eyes, without personal anger, rather with a sense of hopeless frustration. 'It would be such a *waste* if you were to take me back!'

As she struggled to her feet he reached out his hand to her and a look passed between them that caused both to fall silent. And perhaps for the first time since she'd met him Kate had the feeling he'd actually listened to what she'd just said.

'Very well, then.' He nodded. 'Come and prove just how much of a help you're capable of being.' Then he was turning purposefully to stride off

through the mud, wrenching Kate unceremoniously behind him. 'I have just the job for you!'

They were climbing down a narrow embankment
to where flowed what looked like a river in full
spate. Without pausing, Vittorio informed her over
his shoulder, 'Until this morning this was one of
the village streets.' Then he nodded in the direction
in which they were headed. 'What I want you to
help me with is over here.'

They came at last to a tumbledown hut, its hopelessly fragile, wind-besieged walls flapping de-
mentedly in the rain. In the doorway squatted an
elderly woman, her gray hair plastered to her head,
hugging herself with bony arms, quietly moaning
in distress. Vittorio bent briefly with a word of
comfort, then, releasing Kate's arm, he pointed
upwards.

'Her husband,' he explained, pointing to the
figure, perched precariously amid the desolation of
broken banana leaves that had once been the roof
of the little house. 'He climbed up there to escape
the flood and now he can't get down again.' His
brow furrowed as he frowned and his lips thinned
tightly. 'The trouble is, the roof's about to give
way—any minute now, I'd say. We'd better get him
down before it does.'

Kate could see that he was right. The roof was
breaking up before their eyes. She looked at
Vittorio. 'How on earth are we going to do it?'

Vittorio drew her behind him into the single-
roomed hut, then by way of an answer, he squatted
down. 'Climb up on to my shoulders,' he instructed. 'In a sitting position. Let your legs drop

down.' Then, as she obeyed, he gripped her ankles firmly and slowly rose up to his full height again.

He moved gingerly across the sodden floor until they were directly below a huge gap in the roof, stretching his long frame as tall as possible, so that Kate's head poked through the gap. He shouted something in the old man's tongue, then instructed Kate, 'Reach out your hand and grab hold of his. Then hang on as tightly as you can while he slides down towards the hole.'

The rain was beating down on her face, making her eyes screw up as she followed his orders. Then her hand waved blindly in the air for a moment before bony fingers reached out to clutch it. With all her strength, she gripped the old man's hand, feeling his weight bear down on her as he slid towards her. Then through the flapping, broken tendrils of banana leaves, she could see his frail figure inching towards her.

'I'm going to let go now. Grip hard with your legs!' Vittorio shouted to her above the storm. Then, as the old man slithered towards them with gathering momentum, all at once Vittorio had released his grip on her ankles and was reaching out to catch the old man in his arms as he came plummeting at full tilt through the hole.

The very next instant the roof caved in, showering bits of debris all about them, and Kate was clutching at Vittorio's hair as, still perched on his shoulders, she fought to keep her balance. Then he was bending down and lifting her bodily to the floor, while the old couple embraced and showered him with thanks.

Just for a moment he caught Kate's eye. 'Well done,' he told her with a wink.

Unconscious of time, they spent the rest of the day moving from hut to hut and from crisis to crisis, the two of them working together quite naturally, like a practised and well-drilled team. When, at last, the wind dropped and the rain finally ceased, they were at the far end of the village, up to their knees in mud, having just helped a poor stricken family drag their possessions from the mire.

Vittorio caught Kate's eye and glanced at the lightening sky. 'The typhoon's over,' he told her with a smile.

Almost disbelievingly, Kate followed his gaze. 'So it is,' she answered wonderingly. It had seemed as though it would never end.

Vittorio took her by the arm. 'We should get back to the house before it gets dark. There's nothing more we can do for now.'

Then he was leading her through the mud and across the swollen river that earlier that morning had been a narrow, dusty street. And it was only as she stepped into the thigh-high water, feeling the weight of it press like a mountain against her, that Kate finally realised how exhausted she was. It took all her strength to move against the water. She stumbled weakly as her knees folded beneath her.

Some sixth sense caused Vittorio to turn round then, and in an instant he had stepped towards her and scooped her up into his arms. 'Come, *querida*, you're tired out. Put your arms round my neck. Let me carry you.'

Even if she had wanted to, Kate had not the strength to argue. Instead, with a sigh that expressed her gratitude, she let her arms slide loosely round his neck, as he strode off through the water, as though she were a featherweight.

As he moved, his chin brushed roughly against her cheek, and, surreptitiously, she let her eyes flicker over his face—the perfect, high, if mud-spattered cheekbones, the strong straight nose, the crossbow lips, the beguiling indentation in his chin—and the long, black lashes, so thick and silky that she ached to lean forward and lay her lips on them.

Instead, without self-consciousness, she touched her fingers to his cheek and gently rubbed away some of the grime. As the black eyes flicked round to mesh with hers, she was aware of a sense of elation through her tiredness. She smiled at him. 'You should see your face! You look as though you've been dragged through a mud bath.'

'Look who's talking!' He smiled back warmly, making her senses suddenly melt and her heart begin to pound. 'You look as though it was you who dragged me through it!'

As his eyes seemed to linger on her face, Kate turned her head away and closed her eyes, suddenly uncertain of this new easiness between them. Her brain was too tired to figure out why, but something was telling her it should not be so.

By the time they got back to Alfonso and Didi's, night was falling rapidly, the sky inky black. But, at least, in the course of the journey Kate had recovered some of her strength—which was just as well, she observed to herself, as she took in the scene of cheerful chaos that the villa had become.

'Who are all these people?' she blinked at Vittorio, as he set her down in the crowded kitchen, where more than a score of mud-spattered villagers—men, women and children in brave, smiling groups—huddled around the candles and Calor gas lamps.

'I think you'll find they've all been made homeless,' Vittorio explained with a shake of his head. 'They'll be camping out here for the night until their houses can be made habitable again.'

It was at that moment that Didi appeared, carrying a tray of coffee and sandwiches. At the sight of them her face lit up. 'Thank heavens you're both safe!' Then she frowned at Vittorio. 'I swear I couldn't stop her! She just went rushing out!'

Vittorio smiled wryly. 'Oh, don't worry, I know her. Impetuosity's her middle name!'

Didi laid down her tray and hugged Kate warmly. 'You'll never know how glad I am to see you. I was really worried, you know.'

Kate shook her head contritely. 'I didn't mean to worry you. It's just that I can't help doing these crazy things.' She touched Didi's arm. 'What about Alfonso? Is he all right, too?'

Didi nodded cheerfully. 'He's fine, thank heavens. He's upstairs right now getting changed.' She paused to look the two of them up and down, suppressing a giggle as she did so. 'Which is exactly what the pair of you need to do! You'd better go and join the queue for the shower!' She cast a quick glance round the crowded kitchen. 'As you can see, it's going to be a full house tonight. And since we're without electricity—the cables have blown down—we're just going to have to manage as best we can.'

It was a hectic, disorganised, yet enjoyable evening that followed. Didi and Alfonso had offered sanctuary to at least a couple of dozen homeless villagers, including a crew of adorable but noisy children. And somehow they all got showered and fed and were found a corner to bed down for the night.

'I'm afraid we're going to need one of the spare rooms,' Didi told Kate apologetically. 'Alfonso and Vittorio can double up together, and I hope you don't mind sharing a bed with me?'

Kate was quick to assure her that she didn't. 'Right now I'm feeling so exhausted I think I could sleep on a bed of nails!'

But, contrarily, once beneath the sheets, though Didi dropped off almost at once, Kate lay staring, wide-eyed, at the ceiling, knowing that sleep was a long way off. For, though her body was exhausted, her mind was wide awake, remembering and reliving moment by moment all the extraordinary dramatic events of the day.

It had been, without a shadow of a doubt, the most incredible and exciting twelve hours of her life. Scared though she had undoubtedly been at times, she wouldn't have missed the experience for the world. And the most wonderful thing of all about it had been the bond that had grown up between Vittorio and herself.

That was what had affected her most deeply. That was what now kept the sleep from her eyes.

Back there, as they had struggled together against the elements, they had seemed to think and feel as one. Now it was like having her insides torn from her to realise how meaningless those moments had been. By tomorrow the ephemeral bond would be broken and they would be strangers once again. She an impetuous Irish journalist whose path had just happened to cross briefly with his, and he a wealthy Philippine industrialist with a beautiful girlfriend waiting for him.

And that, she now realised with total clarity, was why that sense of closeness had felt so wrong. The feelings that had been bubbling up inside of her, as clear and as optimistic as a mountain stream, were feelings that it was totally inappropriate for her to feel for a man who belonged to another woman.

She tossed and turned, and sighed in dismay, as sleep still refused to carry her away. At this rate she would still be lying here wide-eyed when the bright tropical dawn broke at last through the sky.

In sudden impatience, she pulled back the sheet. There was no point in staying here in bed. She would only end up waking Didi. Perhaps a breath of fresh air would clear her mind and help to blow these foolish thoughts away.

She slid from the bed and pulled off her pyjamas, then quickly slipped on her own blouse and trousers that Didi had kindly prepared for her. Then, barefoot, she padded out into the moonlit hallway, negotiating the sleeping bodies with care, then soundlessly pulled open the front door and stepped out on to the wooden veranda.

Kate sighed as the balmy night air enveloped her, still and warm and heavy and humid, then she leaned against the edge of the veranda and tilted her head up to the sky.

Now that the clouds had finally cleared a huge yellow moon hung low and iridescent, and a carpet of stars, like diamonds strewn on velvet, shimmered and twinkled, almost close enough to touch.

It's so beautiful, she thought with a tug of longing. One of the most beautiful sights I've ever seen. If nothing else, I shall leave this place with a great many unforgettable memories.

She sighed again and shook her head. What a pity that amid all those beautiful memories there was destined forever to be one regret.

'Have you ever seen so many stars?'

A deep voice at her elbow made her spin round, and she blinked and felt her heart lurch in her chest, as she found herself gazing into a pair of black eyes.

It was almost as though he'd dropped down from heaven.

'Vittorio!' she gasped.

CHAPTER SIX

'I COULDN'T sleep either.' Vittorio was smiling as he came to stand alongside her at the edge of the veranda. He let his eyes drift upwards to the stars. 'I bet you don't get nights like this in London.'

Kate laughed softly. 'Nor in Ballyconna. I've never seen a night sky so full of stars.'

He turned to look at her, his dark eyes curious. 'Tell me about Ballyconna,' he urged.

He was wearing his customary faded jeans and an equally faded, once-black T-shirt that fitted snugly over the rippling contours of his magnificently proportioned shoulders and chest. In the moonlight his skin looked dark and lustrous, the black hair as glossy as burnished jet, and the ebony eyes with their fringes of dark lashes seemed to glow with a strange, hypnotic power.

Suddenly wishing she'd had the wisdom to stay in bed, Kate let her eyes drift down to his mouth, with its sensuous, bow-shaped upper lip, then down still further to the dimple in his chin.

'Ballyconna? There's not much to tell. It's really a very ordinary little place.'

'It can't be so ordinary if it produces young women like you.' There was a note of lazy seduction in his voice. He waited till she had raised her eyes to meet his, then asked, 'Do your family still live there?'

'Oh, yes. My Mam and my Dad, my four sisters and one of my brothers. My other brother lives in London with me. He's studying to be a doctor.'

As Kate thought of Liam, warm pride welled up within her and, almost simultaneously, she could hear her brother chastise her. She had misjudged Vittorio. She had thought that Liam would dislike him. And now, on the contrary, she knew that her brother, that infallible judge of character, would think highly of the man before her, perhaps almost as highly as she did herself.

After today, she knew in her heart that all the bad things she had been told about him were untrue.

Vittorio was watching her with close interest. 'You come from an even bigger family than I do. I have two brothers and two sisters. I have the privilege, if you can call it that, of being the eldest.'

Kate laughed in sympathy. 'I know what you mean. I'm the eldest of our brood, too.' She pulled a faintly self-mocking face, remembering the responsibilities of her childhood years when at times she had felt like a stand-in mother. And that sense of responsibility had stayed with her through the years. It was the reason she was here now on the trail of the Cabayan story.

But there was no need for Vittorio to know her sad tale. 'They say that being the eldest makes you grow up quickly,' she smiled. 'Although, I suppose,' she added, teasing, 'it's probably different for a boy.'

'Don't be so sure!' Vittorio smiled wryly, showing a glint of even, perfect white teeth. 'Even now, when all the rest of them are supposedly grown up, too, they still tend to come running straight to me whenever there's a crisis or they need advice!'

Kate watched him, not finding that hard to believe. His strength and his aura of competence and reliability were bound to draw others to him in a storm. To her surprise she found herself secretly envying these unknown brothers and sisters of his. What a comfort and a luxury it must be to have such a man to turn to in one's hour of need!

Vittorio was still watching her, his expression serious. 'You said one of your brothers is studying to be a doctor. Is your father a doctor, too?'

Kate laughed at that. 'Good heavens, no! My father was a truck driver—before the accident.' She frowned a little, aware that she was being drawn into making precisely the revelations she had hoped to avoid. Her private family tragedy would mean nothing to Vittorio. With a small shrug she explained briefly, 'He was crippled in a car crash several years ago. Unfortunately, he hasn't been able to work since.'

'That's very sad.' His tone was sympathetic. 'It's hard for a man to lose his livelihood.'

And for his family, Kate thought, sighing inwardly. Harder than a man like Vittorio could ever imagine.

'All the same,' he was saying, 'he must be very proud of you.' He paused and smiled a lopsided smile. 'I was proud of you this afternoon.'

Kate looked up into his face, all other thoughts dissolving. 'Proud?' she repeated. Had he really said proud?

He nodded. 'Yes, proud. And a little surprised— though only a very little,' he confessed. The fingers of one hand reached out to touch her cheek, sending a dart of electricity up to her scalp. 'Not many girls, especially strangers to this country, would have had the guts to do what you did.'

Suddenly a football was lodged in her throat. She swallowed futilely and just managed to say, 'Guts had really nothing to do with it. I simply did what needed doing.'

'At considerable personal risk,' he begged to remind her, letting his fingers slip round beneath her hair, caressing the warm sensitivity of her neck. 'You could easily have stayed in the house, as I told you to do, and taken care of your own personal safety.' He smiled a crooked smile. 'By the way, those things you said to me while we were wrestling in the mud... You were wrong, you know. I wasn't just angry that you'd disobeyed me. I really was concerned for your safety.'

Part of Kate wanted to step away, to liberate herself from his caress. But a far greater part of her ached to melt against him and surrender to the need he ignited within her.

Hoarsely, she told him, 'I'm sorry I said that. In fact, there are a lot of things I'm sorry I ever said. It's just that I was told so many bad things about you. I should never have listened. I should have judged for myself.'

Vittorio kissed her nose, making her heart leap. 'Does that mean you've revised your opinion of me?'

Kate flushed and nodded. 'But why would people say such things? Ramos, for example. Why would he mislead me? What on earth has he got against you?'

Vittorio silenced her with a touch of his finger. 'Let's not spoil things by talking about Ramos.' Then his fingers slid round to tangle with her hair. 'Let me kiss you, *querida*.' His voice was low and husky. 'All I want is to kiss you and hold you. All day I have been longing for a moment such as this.'

With the gentlest of movements he was drawing her to him, gathering her like eiderdown into his arms. 'You are the most exciting woman I have ever known. Do you know that?' He pressed her close. 'I cannot get you out of my mind. Every moment of the day I find myself thinking of you.'

His fingers in her hair were making her whole body tremble. Sparks of electricity flickered down to her toes. And she only just had time to let out a whimper—more a breathless surrender than a cry of protest—before she felt his grip around her tighten and suddenly his lips were burning down on hers.

She could have wept for the beauty of that kiss, and, even as it melted her bones within her, she knew it was a kiss she would never forget.

For this kiss was like no kiss ever before. It filled her with a sharp, sweet sense of ecstasy that seemed to lift her bodily up to the stars. It felt like dying and waking up in heaven, she found herself musing in distracted euphoria. The overwhelming gentleness and warmth and passion of him seemed to flow from his lips and fill up her soul.

As his mouth possessed hers, erotic and masterful, prising her eager lips apart, every muscle in her body convulsed with longing and a hunger like wildfire ripped through her veins. I must be suffering from jungle fever! one portion of her brain was fighting to rationalise. Never, not even in my wildest imaginings could I have dreamed it possible to feel this way for a man!

One hand was caressing, moving deliciously against her, loosening her blouse from the waistband of her trousers. Then all at once a shiver went through her as his fingers made contact with her warm, naked flesh.

His hand did not move immediately to her breast, but paused, tantalisingly, to caress her midriff. And, simultaneously, his lips slid from her mouth to plant warm, searing kisses on her brow and her neck.

'*Querida, querida* ... How delicious you are. A thousand times sweeter even than I'd dreamed ...'

As he pressed her even closer, making her limbs turn to putty, she could feel his arousal hard against her belly. Then, even as her own hands hovered on his shoulders, uncertain whether she dared embrace him, the hand beneath her shirt was sweeping upwards to claim possession of her breasts.

She was wearing no bra and the sudden naked contact sent a jolt of raw electricity burning through her. As his lips returned to cover hers once more, she heard him murmur, '*Querida, mi amor.*' Then every sense in her entire body was suddenly quite ruthlessly overtaken by the magic that his fingers were working on her breasts.

Greedily, he moved from one to the other, moulding their firm heaviness in the palm of his hand, circling with his fingers the stiff hungry peaks, sending jolts of sheer, exquisite anguish through her.

As his fingers teased, the spiral of longing was tightening almost unbearably in her loins. Wantonly, her body pressed against him. I shall die, she thought desperately, if he stops now.

Perhaps it was the clarity of the signal she was sending him that set off an alarm bell in his head, for all at once his grip around her had slackened and his hand was dropping away from her breast.

'I think we'd better stop there.' His voice was husky, as he adjusted the cream-coloured blouse at her waist. Then, holding her gently, he dropped a kiss on her face. 'It's time each of us went to our own separate beds. Come, *querida*. Let me lead the way.'

On legs of sponge Kate let him take her by the hand and lead her back along the veranda. Then they were picking their way over blissfully sleeping bodies till they came to their respective bedroom doors.

In the half-light of the hallway Kate could barely see his face as he lifted her hand momentarily to his lips. 'Goodnight, *querida*, he bade her softly. 'Sleep well. I wish you pleasant dreams.'

Like an obedient zombie Kate nodded, 'Goodnight.' Then she stepped into the room where Didi was sleeping and silently closed the door behind her.

Sleep well, he had told her. She smiled to herself dreamily. I shall never sleep again as long as I live!

Eventually Kate did sleep, as it turned out. A tranquil and deeply satisfying sleep, scattered with fragments of dreams like flower petals. And when she awoke next morning, she awoke with a start, her mind filled with one certainty as warm as sunlight. She was no longer the same person she had been before. She felt different, light-headed, buoyant and vulnerable.

For something stupendous and quite unforeseeable had happened. She had fallen head over heels in love!

She lay very still in the empty bed, glad that Didi had already risen, leaving her alone in the big, sunny room. For she needed a moment of total privacy to examine this sudden transformation. It could not be physical—though she had not checked, she imagined she must still look pretty much the same!—and yet she could feel, as sure as sunrise, that every atom of her being had been renewed.

It was as though, before, she had merely been existing, whereas now, all at once, she had come alive. The room she lay in, though the shutters were still fastened, seemed brighter and more colourful than any room before. The sheets she lay between felt softer and more silky and there was a scent, like rose blossom, in the air. She could almost hear music drifting to her ears with every soft sigh of the breeze outside.

Kate pinched herself beneath the sheet, just to make certain that she wasn't still dreaming. Could all of this possibly have been brought on by a couple of stolen midnight kisses? Could a few magical moments in Vittorio's arms really have had so profound an effect?

She lay back against her pillows, her body feeling as though it were floating, and gazed, wide-eyed and unseeing, into space. So, this was what love felt like! She had often wondered. It felt like gazing at the world from some peak of the universe.

Yet harsh reality was drawing her earthwards with a bump, for what did she really have to feel so overjoyed about? Love might have finally entered her life and illuminated her soul with its warm, lustrous light, but at the same time fate had treated her cruelly. For the man it had chosen to steal her heart away was a man who was promised to another.

Vittorio de Esquerez belonged to Carmen. Kate had to face it. He could never be hers.

And yet... And yet... All those things he had said. All those whispered endearments as he had held her in his arms. 'You are the most exciting woman I have ever known... I cannot get you out of my mind. Every moment of the day I find myself thinking of you.'

He would not have said these things, surely, if he had not meant them.

Perhaps he did not love Carmen, after all!

Hope stirred within her as she sought to remember the words he had used at dinner the other night. Words that had rung discordantly at the time and had stuck in her head like a fishbone in one's craw.

When Didi had described Carmen as the future Mrs De Esquerez, he had responded enigmatically, 'We are expected to marry.' It had sounded evasive and it had made Kate wonder. But perhaps now she knew the reason for his reticence. Perhaps he was not quite as committed to Carmen as everyone around him believed.'

She jumped from the bed, alight with sudden optimism, suddenly impatient to see him, anticipating the thrill of seeing his face. As soon as she looked at him, she would know if she was dreaming. She would see her destiny revealed in that deep dark gaze.

Kate dressed quickly in her own shirt and trousers and hurried through to the kitchen, her heart beating within her. And there he was, seated at the table, his back to her, as he bent over his breakfast.

He was dressed in one of his customary faded T-shirts that made the sunborn darkness of his arms and neck take on an almost golden sheeny lustre, and endowed the glossy coal-black of his hair, that was pushed back carelessly away from his face, with the deep dark richness of polished gunmetal. And Kate felt for a moment a tremor inside her at the memory of how it had felt in his arms.

'Good morning, *señorita.*' He had sensed her presence and was slowly turning round to greet her. But as the black eyes paused for barely an instant before turning back to the plate before him, Kate felt an anxious tightening within her. She had been expecting a little more warmth than this.

'Good morning,' she answered, her tone falsely cheerful. Sudden fear was replacing her earlier elation. Had last night been a dream, after all? She crossed to the table and sat down opposite him, all at once unwilling to look him in the face. Then in an effort to appear natural she glanced around the kitchen. 'Where is everybody?' she enquired. For there was no sign either of their host and hostess, nor of any of their fellow guests.

'If you're referring to the villagers, they were all up and about hours ago, anxious to get on with rebuilding their homes.' He did not look at her as he answered. Instead, he reached for the coffee-pot and poured himself a cupful, then with a careless, almost contemptuous gesture, he pushed the pot towards Kate. 'I left Alfonso over at the power station,' he added. 'The electricity should be on again within the hour. As for Didi, she's gone to visit one of the families in the village. She said she wouldn't be too long.'

Kate stared miserably at the coffee-pot, feeling a pain in her chest as big as a cathedral and a sense of total desolation. What a fool she had been! Last night had meant nothing. While she, like a fool, had been falling in love with him, he had been amusing himself, purely and simply.

He raised his eyes to her across the table. 'What's the matter? Is something bothering you?' Then as she flushed a little, ashamed at her own transparency, he added, 'I would suggest that you force yourself to have some breakfast. You have rather a long journey ahead of you.'

Kate's eyes snapped up then. Journey? What journey? Then in an instant she remembered. 'Of course. Manila.' Dully, she dropped her gaze again. In her state of euphoria she had forgotten everything, including Vittorio's intention to pack her off back to Manila. Black despondency descended as she asked him, 'What time are Didi and Alfonso leaving?'

He raised his napkin to his lips. 'Alfonso and Didi aren't going to Manila. I'm afraid there's been a change of plan.'

'Not going to Manila?' Kate frowned. 'Why not?'

He made a vague gesture. 'There's too much to do here. The typhoon did quite a lot of damage to the village—though, mercifully, no one's been seriously hurt.' His tone was flat, devoid of sentiment, as though he were explaining a mathematical equation. 'Alfonso couldn't possibly go off and leave the village now, especially since he has no particularly urgent need to go to Manila.'

This news begged more questions than it answered. 'So, what's happening?' Kate queried, genuinely baffled. 'If not Didi and Alfonso, who's taking me back?'

'Nobody's taking you back to Manila.' With a harsh sigh Vittorio tossed down his napkin. 'Unfortunately, it looks as though I have no choice but to take you with me to Cabayan.'

Kate should have felt elated, but all she was aware of was the swift dart of pain that pierced through her heart. He had spoken that 'unfortunately' with such feeling that the cruelty of it took her breath away.

Vittorio smiled thinly. 'You see my dilemma. I can hardly leave you here in Bagu Bayo indefinitely—for at the moment it is quite impossible to tell when Alfonso might be free to travel to Manila. I could postpone my journey south and take you back myself, but I have a feeling my presence in Cabayan is required somewhat urgently.'

He pushed strong, tanned fingers through his thick black hair and pulled an expression of pained resignation. Then the dark brows drew together as he he warned her, 'However, just because I'm taking you along with me, don't think I'm giving you permission to write your article.' He paused deliberately to drain his coffee-cup, then laid it with a sharp click back on its saucer. Steely black eyes held hers for a moment. 'As far as that's concerned, nothing has changed.'

Kate watched mutely as he pushed back his chair and, with a closed expression, rose to his feet. He was absolutely right, of course. Nothing had changed.

Except that as she sat there, white-faced and still, she felt as though her heart had been ripped from her breast. And suddenly the fact that she had won this small victory—however reluctantly, he was taking her to Cabayan—was a totally empty and barren triumph.

For there was only one thing in the world that mattered. One cruel truth that was tearing her apart.

For she could not deny it. It was as clear as crystal.

In spite of all the soft words he had spoken, Vittorio did not care one jot for her.

Within the hour they had said their farewells to Didi and Alfonso and were heading once more into the jungle. By midday they had travelled a good forty miles across terrain made even more difficult by the storm. And by the time the sun at last began to set, according to Vittorio's calculations, they were more than halfway along the road to Cabayan.

Throughout the journey barely a word had been spoken, except when communication was strictly essential. And they had stopped only once—to eat the chicken and rice that Didi had packed for them—and then just long enough to get the food down before setting off on the road again.

Vittorio, of course, had had a good excuse for his silence. The atrocious driving conditions demanded all of his attention, not to mention a large chunk of his energy too.

At least a dozen times an hour—Kate had actually counted them!—he'd been obliged to climb down on to the road to bodily drag some storm-damaged tree from their path or to cut their way clear with his machete where branches had fallen and tangled before them.

Little wonder he'd shown no inclination to chat—although Kate sensed he was grateful for the excuse to remain silent. There was an unfamiliar reserved air about him today.

Guilt, Kate decided. His conscience was bothering him.

For her own part Kate had been glad to be left in peace. It allowed her the opportunity to examine her own thoughts and to come to terms with the tumult in her heart.

Of course, she had been foolish to imagine anything else. Some madness must have briefly overtaken her. For how could she, plain Kate O'Shaughnessy, ever hope to compete with a woman like Carmen for the affections of a man like Vittorio de Esquerez?

She had seen with her own eyes the chic and glamorous Carmen. She should have known what type of female attracted him. Girls like herself, by brutal contrast, were good only for a couple of stolen kisses. They served as a brief and meaningless diversion. A momentary trifle. A passing amusement. They were not the type to be taken seriously. And, above all, they were most certainly not the type a man like Vittorio would ever fall for.

Through her sense of desolation, anger stirred within her. He had treated her as a plaything, spinning false endearments that, just for a moment, had turned her head. No wonder he had been irritated at having to take her with him. He had been planning, no doubt, just to dump her casually and conveniently and forget all about last night.

She stole a glance at his profile, her anger growing. All she was to him now was an inconvenience. An embarrassing reminder of a moment of weakness. And she was a fool. She should have known.

But her anger was futile. It was a waste of energy that would be better directed towards something more positive. Her jaw firmed perceptibly. She straightened a little. What she must concentrate on now was getting her story.

He had said that he still planned to stop her getting it, but once she was in Cabayan there was nothing that would stop her! As her resolution firmed, she began to feel stronger. Her story. That was what she must focus on now. To the exclusion of all else, she must keep it in front of her. She must fill every cranny and corner of her mind with it, so that not a single atom of space was left empty for her grinding, inconsolable sense of grief.

It was late when they finally stopped to pitch camp.

'I'll put up the tent while you prepare supper,' Vittorio commanded, climbing down from the car. And although the brusqueness of his tone momentarily grated on her sensitivities, Kate allowed nothing in her demeanour to give that away. Hadn't she vowed to be totally impervious to him?'

As he went off with the tent, Kate crouched in the car's headlights to set up the little Calor gas stove and opened up a can of sausage and beans. And suddenly she was aware of a striking change in her.

In spite of their awesome isolation—they hadn't passed within miles of another village all day—she felt quite unafraid, her original nervousness of this wild place somehow magically all melted away. In fact, all day she had felt as safe with Vittorio as though she were in the civilised heart of some metropolis.

She pushed the thought away. It was far too positive. And such positive thoughts would only undermine her. Already she could feel a warm glow melt through her as her eyes drifted longingly to his tall, lithe figure, bent now a little as he banged in the tent pegs.

Somehow she must hang on to every shred of antipathy that she was still capable of summoning up against him. Foolishly she had allowed her heart to drift away from its previous safe anchorage of hatred for him. She must cling on for dear life now to her resentment if she was to save herself from being swept away.

A moment later he had finished with the tent pegs and was striding across the rough ground towards her. He came to stand just a few feet away, his nearness, in spite of her fierce resolution, causing Kate's heart to flip over like a pancake.

He glanced down at her. 'Is it nearly ready yet?'

Kate dared not look at him. 'Just another couple of minutes.' She gave the pan a vigorous shake. 'The sausages need a moment to heat through.'

To her dismay, he squatted down beside her and bent over the stove to examine her handiwork. 'Smells good,' he informed her. 'Sausages and beans. Precisely what I'm in the mood for.'

Kate could sense an air of ambivalence about him, as though he could not quite make up his mind how to treat her and had opted for this bland display of politeness as the solution least likely to make waves.

But blandness of any kind did not suit him. His was a temperament of thunderclaps and flashes, of fulminating flares of unfettered passion, of emotions that constantly simmered and bubbled. This passionless display of friendly civility must be grating on his nerves.

It was his conscience, of course, that was causing him to act this way. After all, in a small way, he had been unfaithful to Carmen, and a man of his basically old-world morality was bound to be bothered by such things.

But whereas he appeared in control of his emotions, Kate's poor nerves were stretched like piano wire. Part of her longed to unleash against him all the anger she felt at the way he had misled her. But it would do her no good to let loose such wild passions. On the contrary, it would only do her harm. One spark, she sensed, would only lead to a conflagration. A conflagration she would be unable to control.

'I reckon it must be ready now.' With a closed expression she reached for one of the tin plates that she had laid on the ground beside her and piled it with sausages and beans. Then, without looking at him, she handed the plate to Vittorio. 'Be careful,' she warned him. 'It's very hot.'

'Thank you, *querida*.' He took the plate and sat down just a couple of feet away from her. He arranged himself comfortably, in a cross-legged position, leaning lightly against the trunk of a tree.

Kate spooned a small portion on to her own plate, aware that her hand was suddenly trembling with all the pent-up emotion that bubbled inside her. Initially, she had been hungry, but her appetite had vanished to be replaced instead by a seething anxiety, all the more powerful because she could not quite put a name to it.

It was no good, she just couldn't do what he was doing and act as though last night had never happened. It had affected her deeply, shaken her to her roots. She couldn't just shrug it off like a bout of hiccups.

He was glancing across at her as he chewed his sausages. 'What's the matter? Why aren't you eating?'

Kate flicked him a glance of guarded hostility. 'I'll eat when I'm ready. I'm just waiting for it to cool.'

'But there's nothing on your plate. It's half-empty,' he continued. 'There's barely enough there to satisfy a sparrow.'

'It's enough for me. I'm not terribly hungry.'

'That's what you said at breakfast. And at lunchtime. Is something the matter with you, *querida*?'

What was this? The Spanish Inquisition? This time her hostility was less guarded as she told him tightly, 'If you don't mind, I'll eat exactly as much as I want to eat. My appetite is none of your damned business!'

Vittorio stopped chewing, his brows drew together and for a moment he regarded Kate in silence. 'I fear there is definitely something wrong with you. Such an angry little outburst for no reason. It would appear that your nerves are a little on edge.'

There was a faint inflexion in his voice that made Kate suspect that he was baiting her. She glared across at him, green eyes flashing. How dared he amuse himself at her expense and try to make a fool of her into the bargain? 'There's nothing at all wrong with me,' she informed him unsteadily, finding it almost painful to look him in the eye. 'So, just eat your supper and mind your own business!'

He smiled a little and raised one dark eyebrow, and now there was no doubt that he was mocking her. 'Tell me what it is. I'm a very good listener. Many women have found me a most sympathetic confidant.'

Damn him! Now he was insulting her. By classifying her in the loose category of 'many women', he was subtly but unequivocally assigning her to the lower ranks among those females who had passed through his life. And it was quite unforgivable of him. First he had led her on and now he was insulting her, playing with her emotions as though she were a toy.

Angrily, Kate flung down her plate. 'I've had enough of this stupid conversation!' And she was just about to scramble indignantly to her feet—she would not stick around to be the butt of his cruel jokes!—when, with the speed of a whiplash, he leaned towards her and fingers like steel curled round her wrist.

'Where do you think you're going, *señorita*? I have not finished talking to you yet.'

With one movement he had laid aside his plate, caught her other wrist with his free hand and dragged her on her knees to kneel beside him. His eyes narrowed imperiously. 'Don't you know it's rude to get up and leave in the middle of a conversation?'

'We weren't having a conversation! I'd said all I have to say to you!'

'I think not, *querida*.' He shook his dark head. 'You were about to tell me what it is that's wrong with you.'

'Nothing's wrong with me! How many times do I have to tell you?'

'As many as you like. But I shall never believe it.' He tightened his grip, drawing her closer, so that she had to tense sharply to avoid falling against him. The black eyes drove into hers without mercy. 'Since you are so reticent, perhaps I should answer for you. You see, I happen to know very well what it is that is causing this bad mood of yours.'

He had her pinned alongside him like a flag to a flagpole. She could struggle all she liked but she could not break free. And suddenly Kate's heart was flapping with pure panic. Her insides felt heavy, as though turned to cold clay.

He jerked her towards him. 'Shall I tell you, *querida*? Shall I tell you what it is that has been bothering you all day?'

Kate pursed her lips in futile defiance. 'Kindly just let me go,' she implored.

'Surely not without first clearing up this little mystery? I'm sure we would both feel much better with that out of the way.'

'Just let me go!' Kate felt like weeping. He had her completely at his mercy, and he had no mercy, no mercy at all. 'I keep telling you there's nothing wrong with me. Why do you refuse to believe me?'

Vittorio smiled darkly. 'Do not lie. Why do you insist on hiding from the truth when the remedy to your woes can so easily be supplied?'

He paused for an instant, making her heart squeeze, then deliberately he released his hold on one wrist and slid his free hand round to the back of her neck. His fingers were in her hair, forcing her closer. Then the black eyes flashed as he bent to kiss her.

That was when something inside Kate exploded. She flung herself at him, claws unleashed, like a wildcat. Her fists pummelled his chest, her hands tore at his hair, her nails dug into his hard, cool flesh.

'You bastard! I hate you!' she shrieked at him, her eyes suddenly bright with tears of fury, her whole body trembling with the passion of her anger. 'I hate you! I detest you! How dare you play your games with me?' Helpless sobs of anguish shook her. She longed to tear him apart with her bare hands.

But she had not the strength. She could barely hurt him. And suddenly her flailing fists were pinioned as Vittorio grabbed hold of her and threw her to the ground.

'Such a waste of passion, *querida mia*.' His eyes flashed strangely as they burned into hers. 'But a fight is not really what you want, I am thinking. What you really want is this.'

And a shudder tore through her fevered, struggling body as he leaned against her and bent to kiss her.

It was a fierce, ungentle, masterful kiss. A kiss that scorched and tore at Kate's senses. Its fury consumed her, a bushfire through her senses. She could not think. She could not breathe.

His mouth ground against hers, prising her lips open. 'This is what you have been wanting, is it not, *querida*?' His words were a taunt, his tongue a sweet torture as it flicked like a serpent's against her teeth. His breath was warm and thick against her. 'Admit it, *querida*. You were pining for this.'

His hand in her hair, fingers driving against her scalp, was sending shivers of sensation tingling down her spine, and Kate could feel her suddenly limp body tremble as his free hand began to tug her blouse open.

He no longer held her prisoner by the wrists and yet she made not the slightest move to escape him. There would be no point, she told herself weakly. His strength is far superior to mine. Yet that argument, she knew, was merely an excuse. The truth was he was right, she had wanted this.

But not like this, not this contemptuous assault, not this arrogant attempt to humiliate and degrade her. As he snatched open the last few buttons of her blouse, his weight pinning her to the ground as his hand sought her breast, she was aware of a tear sliding softly down her cheek. 'Please, Vittorio. Don't treat me this way.'

She had whispered too softly for him to have heard her, and yet even as she drew breath to protest with more vigour she could sense a sudden change come over him, as dramatic as though someone had thrown a switch.

The lips that consumed her did not grow more gentle and the fingers that were prising her breasts free from her bra had lost none of their burning greedy urgency. And yet what had begun as an angry assault had turned into something very different. There was an honest raw passion in that hard devouring mouth of his and the hand that moulded her swollen breast was intent all at once on administering pleasure, not punishment.

He raised his eyes to look at her. 'How beautiful you are. How beautiful, how perfect, *querida*.' Somehow, he had undone the fastening of her bra, exposing her breasts with their pink erect nipples. He let his hands sweep over them, sending darts of pleasure through her, then paused to graze the aching peaks between his fingers.

As she gasped at the spasm of sensation that shot through her, he smiled and bent to kiss her face. 'I want to pleasure you, my darling. I want to make you mad for me, just as you make me mad for you.'

Then he buried his face against her bosom, inviting her to tangle her fingers in his hair, and as his weight bore down on her she could feel his excitement rampant and hard against her loins. A thrill went through her and a sudden fierce longing that caused her all at once to arch her back and press her hips wantonly against him. For suddenly she longed to feel that hardness thrusting like a rapier between her thighs.

'Vittorio... Vittorio...' She breathed his name like a prayer as he bent all at once to capture one nipple firmly, excruciatingly, between his teeth. And as he proceeded with his torment, making her bones melt within her, Kate's hands were sliding beneath his T-shirt to caress the firm hard flesh of his shoulders and chest.

'*Mi dulce* Katharine.' He drew his face level and gazed long and deep into her eyes. 'How I long to make love to you, to make you mine totally. And I can feel it is what you long for, too.'

He let his hand drift over her, caressing her bosom, then sliding down towards her waist. His fingers tugged at the button of her trousers, then in one deft movement slid down the zip. And Kate could feel her flesh jump at the touch of his fingers as they moved down below the top of her briefs.

For one heart-stopping moment, she dared to hesitate. She wanted him with her body and her heart and her soul. And that was the vital difference between them. For he wanted her with his body alone.

With a rough sigh she drew his hand away. She shook her head slowly. 'No, Vittorio!'

He belonged to Carmen. And however much Kate might long for his possession, she could never give herself to a man who bore the brand of another woman.

He had the grace, at least, not to argue. Instead, he carefully drew up the zip of her trousers and bent to kiss her softly on the mouth. 'You are right, of course. We have not yet had dinner.' He was making a joke of it. He smiled down at her. 'One must never make love on an empty stomach.'

But though she smiled in response as he moved away from her and Kate began to do up the buttons of her blouse, inwardly she was weeping. What folly to have fallen in love with a man for whom she would never be more than a fleeting diversion. Something to be enjoyed and then forgotten. A secret, sordid peccadillo.

And suddenly a great void opened in her heart and she cursed with a sense of bottomless despair the cruel whim of fate that had brought them together.

CHAPTER SEVEN

IT WAS a huge relief to Kate when they came to Cabayan at last. After two days trapped alone in Vittorio's company she was starting to fall apart at the seams.

There had been no repeats of that previous flight of passion and he had never again attempted any similar seduction. If he had, without a doubt, Kate would have resisted him. On that point now her resolve was strong.

Yet, in spite of his new reticence, he continued to trouble her, for he was like a weather-vane, forever changing without warning, one moment blowing hot, the next blowing cold. And it cut like a knife when he acted coolly towards her, for she could tell it was calculated on his part. Deliberately, he was driving a wedge between them.

For beyond the deeper emotional discrepancies—Kate's hopeless love against his intermittent lust for her—that spiritual closeness that had grown between them on the day of the typhoon had never really disappeared.

During the occasional brief interlude when the barriers were lowered the empathy between them buzzed like electricity. They would find themselves talking, laughing, joking, like the lovers they had so nearly become.

Then all at once their eyes would mesh together and the spirit of Carmen, never-mentioned but ever-present, would rise up between them, a chilling reminder. And their eyes would fall away, his in guilt, hers in sorrow, and the barriers would spring into place once again.

So it was that as, on the third day of their journey, the Nissan bumped its way into the camp at Cabayan, Kate put up a silent prayer of thanks that, for the moment at least, her ordeal was over. With other people around her, other things to think of, perhaps this pain in her heart would ease off a little.

Cabayan was nothing like Bagu Bayo. At first glance there was no sign of a village as such, just a cluster of large tents in a clearing of the jungle, with a couple of four-wheel drives parked outside.

'This is Professor Flynn's expedition head-quarters,' Vittorio explained to her as they drew to a halt alongside one of the tents. He pointed beyond the clearing into some trees. 'The village proper is over there.'

Kate squinted as she followed his pointing finger. All she could see were some huts built of bamboo and banana leaves. She glanced back at Vittorio. 'It looks very primitive.'

He smiled at her wryly. 'It is,' he assured her.

Professor Flynn turned out to be the perfect image of an absent-minded academic. A wiry little Australian with a bushy red beard, dressed in a dishevelled grey safari suit, he had about him the faintly comic air of one whose thoughts are per-petually distracted. Yet an undeniable, needle-sharp intelligence shone out at the world through his brilliant blue eyes.

And he was indubitably delighted to set eyes on Vittorio. 'My good friend! What a lovely surprise!' The tall Spaniard had scarcely stepped through the tent flap before Flynn was hurrying forward to slap him on the back. 'You couldn't have come at a more propitious time!'

'I had a feeling you were going to say that.' Warmly, Vittorio shook hands with the older man. Then he turned with a smile in Kate's direction. 'Meet Miss Kate O'Shaughnessy,' he invited. 'A reporter from *Deadline* magazine in London.'

Kate flicked him a surprised look as she stepped forward politely to shake hands with the Australian professor. By introducing her as a journalist, he had virtually legitimised her purpose for being here.

The bright blue eyes of the professor widened. 'A journalist, you say?' he enquired with interest. 'I think you'll find no shortage of stories here.' Then he turned his attention back to Vittorio. 'I have to admit you were right all along. I wish I'd had the sense to listen to what you told me.'

Exactly what he meant by that Kate was going to have to wait to discover. As they all sat down on the makeshift benches that were the only seating in the professor's little 'office', a young man suddenly appeared and was introduced as Giles, Flynn's assistant.

'My right-hand man,' Flynn generously acknowledged, as Giles busied himself making coffee in one corner. 'As you'll have gathered, I'm a bit of an organisational disaster. Young Giles here keeps things running smoothly.'

The fair-haired Giles grinned as he handed round cups, took one himself and sat down on one of the benches. 'I do all the boring, routine stuff, simply to justify my presence. The professor's the one who's running the show. Believe me, he's the expert.'

Flynn shook his head and stared into his coffee. 'An expert in the field of anthropology, perhaps, but alas not in the field of human nature.' He raised his eyes and glanced across at Vittorio. 'As I was saying, I should have listened to what you told me. I should never have got involved with that man.'

Vittorio leaned forward a little in his seat, long fingers circling his steaming coffee-cup. 'What's up?' he enquired in an even tone. 'Are you having trouble with Ramos?'

Flynn exhaled slowly, in an expression of frustration. 'Not directly with Ramos. With one of his men here—though I've no doubt Ramos himself is behind it.' He sat back in his seat and shrugged dishevelled shoulders. 'The trouble is I'm no good at handling such problems. I haven't a clue how to go about it.'

'Then you'd better tell me what's going on.' A terse note had crept into Vittorio's voice. 'I'm an old hand at dealing with Ramos.'

Flynn shook his head. 'It's really quite shocking. To tell you the truth, I can hardly believe it.' He shook his head again and tugged at his beard. 'Ramos's men are supposed to be helping us—but now I've discovered they've been faking the evidence!'

'I'd believe anything of our old friend Ramos,' Vittorio assured him with a hollow laugh. Then instantly his expression sobered. 'Faking the evidence how?' he asked.

Flynn sighed. 'It was young Giles here who first became suspicious. He was sure there was something funny going on between Ramos's number one man down here, Eddie—he's our interpreter, among other things—and Taku, one of the head men of the tribe. We don't know if any money has actually changed hands, but we've reason to believe that money has been promised—in exchange for the co-operation of the tribe in inventing all sorts of totally inaccurate details.'

Flynn sighed again at the enormity of what he was recounting and his blue eyes filled with a look of betrayal as he gathered himself together and carried on, 'As you know, the tribe have been isolated for centuries, and though they're undoubtedly backward, in their own way they've evolved. They're far from being the Stone Age creatures that Ramos and his men are trying to make them out to be.

'Would you believe,' he demanded of Vittorio, 'we've actually uncovered some Stone Age implements—primitive weapons and tools for cooking—that I'm ninety-nine per cent certain have been planted? We even have reason to suspect that Eddie and his cronies have been instructing the tribal elders in various colourful rites and rituals—rain dances and all sorts of ridiculous nonsense—that I would swear have never been a part of their culture.' His expression was pained. 'How could they?' he beseeched. 'They're making a mockery of all my careful research.'

Kate had listened to every word with mounting horror—horror at herself—and mingled shame. Now she understood why Ramos had lied about Vittorio. As the villain himself it made a perverse kind of sense for him to try to blacken the name of the man who was out to stop him.

She shot Vittorio a look of mortification. How could she have believed Ramos's lies?

In the flicker of an eyelid he had understood and absolved her. He took a mouthful of his coffee and turned to the subject of Ramos. 'I'll tell you right now what he's up to. The reason he's embroidering the facts is to make a more colourful story for public consumption. As I told you, Ramos isn't the least bit interested in serious scientific research. All he wants is a commercial product, something he can exploit and make some money out of. And if it doesn't exist, he's quite prepared to invent it. He doesn't give a damn about the truth.'

Flynn sucked in his breath. 'And to think that I refused to listen when you warned me not to get involved with the man!' He pulled a wry face at his own gullibility. 'But he seemed so convincing, I believed he was serious.' He glanced across at Kate. 'Have you met this man Ramos?'

Kate nodded. 'Yes, I've met him,' she admitted. 'And you're right, he's a most convincing liar. But, don't worry,' she smiled, casting a quick glance at Vittorio. 'I'm sure Señor de Esquerez will sort it all out for you.'

As Vittorio raised one faintly amused eyebrow at this spontaneous declaration of total faith in him, Flynn turned to fix him with anxious blue eyes. 'Will you?' he entreated.

'It'll be my pleasure,' Vittorio assured him. 'Don't worry, Professor. I'll do everything I can to assist you.'

The relief on Flynn's face was almost palpable. 'I'm most grateful to you, Señor de Esquerez. But I think I should warn you, certain threats have been made as a warning that it would be unwise to interfere.'

'Is that so?' Vittorio smiled, as though this unsavoury piece of information simply added to his enthusiasm for the task ahead. 'In that case, I must be sure to tread carefully,' he observed, his smile broadening wickedly as he elaborated, 'but not as carefully, I promise you, as Ramos. He and his gang would be well advised to say a prayer before they take another step.'

It was all clear now. Kate even understood why Ramos had been so reluctant to provide her with guides. The tribe, for whom he had such plans, were evidently not quite ready yet for public exposure. No doubt they were in need of a little more rehearsing before they became totally convincing in their Stone Age personas!

As she lay awake in her sleeping bag that night, housed in solitary splendour in Professor Flynn's 'office', Kate reflected wryly on her own gullibility that had virtually been equal to that of the professor. For although, on the evidence of her own observations, she had come to realise for herself the truth about Vittorio, it had never for one moment crossed her mind that Ramos himself might be guilty of deception.

She shuddered in the darkness at her own naïveté. If things had gone differently, it was perfectly possible that she herself would have fallen for the Stone Age story. Presented with such a plum, she would have found it hard to resist, especially when Ramos had the 'evidence' and of the only two men likely to dispute these findings—Vittorio and the worthy, but unworldly professor—one had been billed as an unscrupulous exploiter with dark ulterior motives of his own, while the other was clearly not up to the task of publicly defending the truth.

More than likely she would have taken the evidence at face value—as indeed would any other journalist, she reckoned. She would have written up a story to present to her public that was nothing but a pack of lies.

So now to her other feelings for Vittorio was added an unexpected debt of gratitude. Though it had not, of course, been his intention to do so, he had protected—and saved—her professional honour!

She turned over wearily and pulled the sleeping bag around her. Vittorio, Vittorio... Her heart bled at the thought of him. He had flown into her life with the power of a meteorite, flooding her heart and her soul with his splendour. Yet destiny had decreed that he must fly on without her, leaving her alone and forever changed.

She thought of the men she had known in the past, none of whom had made any lasting impression. They had come and gone and she had scarcely noticed. Certainly, she had not cared.

But it was Liam who had warned her, 'One day there'll be a man who'll sweep you off your feet when you least expect it and set your heart amid the stars in heaven.'

Only she had not believed him.

And now it had happened.

And all the way from heaven was a long way to fall.

Kate closed her eyes and hugged her arms around her, as though to contain her terrible misery—yet knowing that it was uncontainable. Endless. Unstoppable. Beyond her control. Creeping through her being like blood through a bandage.

If only she had never met him.

If only there had been no Carmen.

At least one good thing had come out of all this chaos. Kate was able to go ahead with her story.

Vittorio had not actually given his permission, but neither had he tried to stop her. Over the next two days, in fact, she barely saw him and passed not a moment alone in his company. He was busy alternately with the professor and with Ramos's henchman, the man called Eddie. So, chaperoned for the most part by the obliging Giles, Kate simply took the opportunity to acquaint herself with the village and its people.

And the more she learned about the tribe of Cabayan the more excited she became about her story.

'What would you like to see happening to the tribe?' she enquired of Professor Flynn one afternoon when she managed to get him to herself for an hour. 'What sort of plans do you have for them?'

The red-bearded professor considered for a moment. 'One must always tread very carefully,' he told her. 'These people have been isolated for so long that any ill-thought-out alterations to their way of life could do them quite immeasurable harm.

'That is why,' he smiled, 'I would suggest that on that particular subject, Señor de Esquerez is the man to talk to. Although he's not an anthropologist, he has more practical experience than I do. As I suppose you know, his company has already been involved in a number of very similar projects. The people he's used to working with are not quite so backward, but the problems he's faced are not so very different.'

Kate nodded, trying to quell the sudden palpitations that just the mention of Vittorio's name had awakened. 'Yes, I've seen one of his projects—at Bagu Bayo. I was very much impressed.'

Flynn nodded in agreement. 'He's done a marvellous job—though, of course, very few people know of his work. Ever since that disaster with the youth project in Manila, he's tended to keep a very low profile.'

A sudden bell went off in Kate's head. 'I heard about that—but what exactly happened?'

'You won't mind my saying this, I hope?' Flynn pulled an apologetic face. 'But I'm afraid some of the more disreputable members of your profession turned the whole thing into a circus, just because a big name like Esquerez was involved. Señor de Esquerez was so incensed that he put round a story that he was withdrawing from the project. It seemed the only way to get the whole thing back to normal and stop any more damage being done to the people he was trying to help.'

Kate blinked at him. 'It was only a story? He didn't really pull out at all?'

'Absolutely not. He remained very much involved with the project in secret. Of course, he came in for a lot of flak from the media for supposedly reneging on his promises, as well as for his outspoken criticisms of the media themselves, but his strategy worked as far as the project was concerned, though it didn't do much for his relations with the Press. He's been subjected to something of a vendetta from some quarters. Some people

never forgave him for some of the things he said
about those journalists.'

Flynn paused and grinned approvingly at her. 'I
believe you're the first journalist he's dealt with
since then. 'You're very lucky. He must trust you.'

Kate smiled a wry smile. If he did, she did not
deserve it. Right from the start she had condemned
him on hearsay. She had listened to those stories
about him in Hong Kong, told to her by fellow-
journalists, never suspecting for one moment that
the people telling the stories might have some personal axe to grind. And now, for the gross injustice
she had done him, she felt nothing but a raw and
bitter sense of shame.

'He's quite a man,' the professor was telling her,
never guessing at how profoundly his listener agreed
with him. 'I made a very big mistake indeed when
I turned down his offer to fund my expedition.'

At Kate's look of mild surprise he went on to
explain, 'I had two offers of funding, you see. One
from Ramos and one from Esquerez—and although
Esquerez's was the more generous, I plumped for
Ramos, because he was less interested in asking me
questions.'

He tugged his beard impatiently, reflecting on his
lack of judgement. 'At our interview, Esquerez gave
me the third degree. He wanted to know every single
detail of how I planned to set up the expedition.
Stupidly, at the time I resented that, I saw it as an
intrusion. It was only later that I realised he had
every right and that the only reason he did it was
because he cared about these people.'

The bright blue eyes were grateful as he added,
'I realise that even more strongly now that he's
come all this way to bail me out. He warned me

I'd have trouble with Ramos—but I wouldn't have blamed him if he'd just washed his hands of me.'

'Vittorio's not the type just to wash his hands,' Kate came in instantly to assure him. He's like me, he gets involved, she added to herself, wishing she didn't find the truth of that quite so painful. It was cruel to have so much in common with a man when his future and her own were destined forever to remain separate.

Kate spent that evening, after dinner with Giles and the professor, squatting on her sleeping bag in her private 'bedroom', sorting out the pile of notes she had made. She had just about everything she needed now for a piece, she felt certain, she could really be proud of. But Flynn had been right. She really needed to talk to Vittorio to make her article complete.

She sighed and laid the notes aside, aware of a tightening in her breast. It was possible, of course, that he might refuse to co-operate. He might even try to block her story altogether. He must have known what she was up to over the past couple of days, as she prowled about the village, notebook in hand, and he had never made any effort to stop her, but then neither had he formally given her his blessing. If he proved difficult she must find a way to persuade him.

Kate suppressed a bitter laugh and closed her eyes. How sensibly she had honed down her aspirations! The best she dared to hope from him now was that he might deign to grant her an interview. Quite a climbdown from a couple of days ago when she had thought he might love her and her dreams had been boundless. For one moment she had seemed to see her future in his eyes. For one moment he had carried her heart to paradise.

But now, with a sharp thud, it was over.

More fool me for being taken in, Kate told herself with a flash of impatience. After all, you always knew about Carmen. It was sheer madness to expect anything else.

She was just about to start getting undressed when she heard the sound of footsteps outside. As the footsteps stopped, she held her breath. If it was Giles come to offer her a nightcap, as he had so thoughtfully done the night before, she would pretend, in spite of the still-glowing gas lamp behind her, to be asleep. But the voice that spoke to her now through the zipped-up tent flap most assuredly was not Giles's.

'*Señorita*, are you awake?'

Kate swallowed and cursed beneath her breath, wishing the lamp were already extinguished. Giles, undoubtedly, would have accepted her silence as indicating that she had fallen asleep. But the man whose profile she could make out now, etched in hard lines against the canvas, she knew with total certainty would simply call her bluff.

She stepped towards the tent door. 'Just a minute.' Then with a faintly unsteady hand she reached for the zip opening. What was he doing here at this time of night? What subtle torture lay in store for her now?

Against the light of the moon that shone tonight like a huge silver guinea high in the sky, the head of black hair, swept back from his brow, was shot with moving quicksilver lights. Vittorio bent towards her, one hand against the tent frame. 'I'm sorry to disturb you,' he told her, watching her, 'but I didn't have a chance to speak to you earlier.'

Kate shivered a little, inwardly, at his nearness. 'That's all right,' she told him. 'I wasn't asleep.'

'I just came to tell you that we're leaving tomorrow. Heading back north to Manila.'

'I see.' She hesitated. 'So soon?'

He smiled at that. 'Don't tell me you want to stay? Don't tell me you've developed an affection for Cabayan?'

'Not exactly,' she answered, though it was not quite true. She had scarcely been aware of it happening, but she had indeed developed an attachment to the place. To Cabayan, to Bagu Bayo, to the Philippines in general. It sounded foolish, but she would miss them.

And then, of course, there was the agony of knowing that the sooner they returned to Manila the sooner she and Vittorio would be parted forever.

Ice touched her heart just at the thought of it, but she kept her tone steady as she told him, 'I'd just thought you might be staying longer.'

'No need.' He shrugged his strong broad shoulders, ripplingly exposed beneath the faded, sleeveless T-shirt. 'I've completed the business that I came for.'

'You mean the business about Ramos? You've sorted it all out?'

'As good as. It's been a highly productive couple of days. Eddie, of course, has been a great deal of help. He's more or less confessed to everything. But then, after I'd turned over his belongings and come up with some highly revealing papers and things from Ramos, he didn't really have a great deal of choice.'

Vittorio smiled with relish, making Kate smile with him. 'I don't anticipate a great deal of resistance from Ramos either. In face, once I've explained in detail my personal plans for him—namely his arrest and the curtailment, once and for all, of all his dishonest business enterprises—I suspect he'll collapse like a house of cards.'

Kate laughed out loud at the undisguised devilment that twinkled from the jet-black eyes. 'I suspect you're right,' she agreed with humour. 'Judging by the last confrontation I witnessed, I can't see poor old Ramos putting up much of a fight.'

And the minute she'd said it she wished she hadn't—for instantly her words took her flying straight back to their very first meeting at Ramos Worldwide. Her eyes drifted down to the cleft in his chin, as a pain like a red-hot knife tore through her. That was the very first time he'd kissed her. And now he would never kiss her again.

There was the faintest pause, no more than a heartbeat. Was it possible, she wondered, that he remembered, too? Then he was saying, 'But, *señorita*, what about you? Have you finished all you came for?'

'You mean my story for *Deadline*?' Her green eyes brightened. His question had definitely not hinted at any further opposition. 'I've done most of the research I'll need,' she told him. 'There's really just one more thing I need...'

As she hesitated just a fraction before asking if he would do the interview, he detached himself from the tent pole against which he had been leaning and stuck his hands into the pockets of his jeans. 'If we're going to continue this conversation, you ought to invite me inside, you know.'

He nodded towards the beam of light from the gas lamp that shone out through the tent flap and into the darkness behind him. 'If you're not careful that light is going to attract a lot of very unwelcome visitors.'

Kate grimaced with understanding. She had quite forgotten the insects that the light from the lamp would attract. 'You're right, you'd better come inside,' she offered, although she would really rather he had stayed outside. Even before he had stepped through the tent flap she could feel the walls of the tent close in around her.

'So, what is this other thing you want?' He seemed to fill the interior with his strong dark presence, as he stood there before her, his hands still in his pockets, the planes of his face thrown into dramatic relief by the flickering blue light of the Calor gas lamp.

'You said there was just one more thing you needed,' he prompted, as she just stood there, staring at him, suddenly unable to answer, fighting back a near-irresistible urge to fling herself into his arms and never let him go.

With an effort Kate pulled herself together. 'Yes, yes. That's right.' She cleared her throat. 'I just wanted to ask you if you might be prepared to answer a couple of questions for me?'

'You mean an interview?'

'An interview, yes. I think it would be helpful. It was Professor Flynn's idea,' she apologised.

The black eyes beneath the straight black brows regarded her in silence for a moment. Then he said, slowly, his tone thoughtful, 'I'd be only too happy to help you...if I could be sure of what type of article you were planning.'

'Oh, you needn't have any worries about that!' Kate lost not a second in reassuring him. 'What I'm planning is something serious and low-key—not the sort of exploitative stuff you disapprove of.'

'You're sure of that?'

'Absolutely sure. You have my solemn guarantee. I told you, *Deadline*'s a serious magazine.'

'Yes, you did.' He smiled as he watched her, yet there was a strange look in his eyes. With a sigh he withdrew his hands from his pockets. 'In that case you shall have your interview,' he told her.

There was a moment of electric silence as they just stood there, looking into one another's eyes. Then Kate found her voice. 'Thank you,' she murmured.

'Don't thank me.' He smiled ambiguously. 'Just make sure you write a damned good story. It's the least you owe yourself after all the trouble you've gone to get it.'

He paused for a moment, his eyes travelling over her, studying with unhurried candour the strong yet feminine delineation of her features—the wide green eyes, the firm nose and mouth, set off in a halo of red-gold curls.

Then, with an unexpected movement, he stepped towards her and Kate's bursting heart seemed to stop within her as one hand reached out to touch her face. The black eyes narrowed. 'When we return to Manila, do you intend to fly straight back to London?'

Why was he asking? Kate hesitated, frowning. 'I don't really know yet,' she answered truthfully.

'So, there's a possibility you might be staying on for a few days? Or maybe even longer?' he enquired.

Kate's heart was ticking nervously inside her. What was he getting at? 'A few days, perhaps,' she answered uncertainly. 'I doubt it would be any longer than that.'

'A few days would be enough.' He smiled suddenly, a smile that sent the blood rushing through her veins. The fingers in her hair were caressing her scalp, then sliding down, shiveringly, to the back of her neck.

Kate's mouth had gone dry. 'Enough for what?'

'For you and I to get together.' Again the smile. Her blood was on fire. 'Whatever you do, you must promise me, *querida*, that you will not return to London without telling me in advance?'

Kate stared at him blankly for a moment, then nodded. She would have promised him anything he cared to ask for.

He drew her a little closer, his hands around her shoulders. 'Try to understand. Now is not the time. Let us wait until we are back in Manila.'

He held her against him, his hands caressing her hair, his voice low as though he were talking to himself. And the only thing Kate was capable of understanding was the searing sensuality of his hips against hers and the way the blood was pounding through her veins.

Then he bent to kiss her, his lips warm and erotic, reducing her poor, aching heart to cinders. And as she clung to him, trembling, she died a thousand deaths. She had believed she would never again feel his kiss and suddenly she realised that would have killed her.

He drew away gently. 'Goodnight, *querida.*' And a moment later, as with one final caress, he was stepping away, back through the tent flap, suddenly all Kate's dreams were reawakening, spinning in her head as sweet as candy floss.

Next morning when the camp awoke Eddie and his four-wheel drive had gone missing.

'It makes no difference,' Vittorio shrugged, as he loaded their things into the back of the Nissan. He held up a bag containing the evidence he had gathered—papers, telexes, phoney Stone Age relics—and laid it carefully beside the rolled-up tent. 'He's probably hoping to get to back to Manila before us to warn Ramos that I'm coming after him. But there's no place for Ramos to hide any longer. This time I shall see to it that his misdeeds catch up with him.'

It had been arranged that Giles would accompany them back to Manila—he had business to see to on behalf of the professor—and the addition of a third person on the long journey north was something Kate had felt unexpectedly grateful for. For as soon as her elation of the previous night had subsided, with a sickening jolt, she had returned to her senses.

It had taken only a moment of rational reflection to unravel the mystery of what Vittorio had been saying last night. He had told her that he wanted to see her in Manila, that he wanted to spend some time with her, and it did not require the mental capacity of an Einstein to figure out what he had in mind.

What he was clearly proposing was a brief sexual fling before she went flying back to London.

Her initial reaction, as the truth sank in, had been anger, outrage and total rejection. A brief affair was not what she wanted. That he should make her such an offer was offensive and demeaning.

And yet... And yet... It was all he had to give her. He wasn't free to offer anything else. And perhaps, she wondered, secretly appalled at herself, a few days of love would be better than nothing.

At least I would have something to remember, she told herself bitterly, fighting back tears. And I shall never again want a man as I want Vittorio. I shall never love another as I love him.

Her mind ground round in interminable circles, and yet before they reached Manila she must decide. Which was why it was such a relief to learn that Giles was coming with them on the long journey back. His presence would allow her space. It would give her an opportunity to think. And, above all, it would prevent Vittorio from repeating his offer and forcing her hand.

As they said their farewells to Professor Flynn, Kate was ready to climb into the back of the Nissan, leaving the front passenger seat to Giles. Let the two of them get on with their man-talk, she was thinking. I'll just hunch in the back and keep myself to myself.

But Vittorio intervened. 'No, *querida*, you get in the front. And bring your pen and notepad with you,' he instructed. 'We can conduct this interview of yours *en route*. If nothing else, it'll help to pass the time.'

Kate obeyed, seeing a sudden advantage. With this final interview she had done all her groundwork. She would have all she needed to write her story. And were she to decide to turn down

Vittorio's offer she would have no need to see him again—for if she turned him down she would want to escape immediately.

Just the thought of that caused a flutter of panic. Never, for all the days of her life, to set eyes on his beloved face again? The breath left her body. How would she survive?

But she must find a way to survive without him, for sooner or later, whatever she decided, the moment of parting must eventually come. Pain tore through her. Better later than sooner. Surely it would not be a sin to steal a few days more?

She pushed the thought away. This decision would destroy her. Long before Manila, she would be a mental wreck.

The journey, in fact, proved almost enjoyable. The three of them got on remarkably well together, passing the hours of bumping through the jungle playing word games and telling each other jokes and stories.

As Kate climbed into her sleeping bag on their second night, she glanced round the little tent she had once shared with Vittorio and listened to the sound of murmuring male voices coming from the bigger tent, provided by Giles, pitched just a metre or so away from her own. If only they need never return to Manila, but could stay here forever in a kind of time warp. Then she need never make up her mind, nor ever have to say goodbye.

They re-entered Manila on the morning of the third day.

Since dawn they had been driving through the steamy silent jungle, then all at once, as they approached the sprawling suburbs, they were surrounded by a bright cacophony of noise. Exotically-painted jeepneys, the capital's mini-buses, with their cargoes of passengers and squawking chickens were hurtling by on either side. Horns blared, drivers yelled and grubby-looking urchins dodged through the traffic selling newspapers and bunches of flowers.

It was back to the real world with a bump, Kate thought ruefully. And in the real world people had to make decisions. The trouble was she had still not made hers.

Giles had told them he'd be staying at the Manila Hotel. 'So I'll drop Giles off first,' Vittorio informed them, 'then I'll carry on to Kate's hotel.'

Which gave her approximately fifteen minutes, Kate calculated in panic, to make up her mind. For he was bound to broach the subject of this affair he had proposed as soon as he had her on her own.

But it was utterly hopeless. Her poor demented mind was still going round in circles when, what seemed like a matter of seconds later, they were drawing up before the Manila Hotel.

Vittorio climbed out to help Giles find his bag, and the two men were so engrossed in what they were doing that neither of them noticed the slender, elegant beauty who had emerged from the main door of the hotel and was gliding slowly down the steps towards them. Kate, however, noticed her instantly. She felt her heart stop dead in her chest.

Of all people in the world to bump into! The girlfriend of the man with whom, at that very moment, Kate was contemplating an affair!

For that was who it was. There could be no mistaking Carmen.

A moment later the girl was calling out his name and Vittorio was swinging round with a smile on his lips. Then he was striding towards her, flinging his arms around her, almost lifting her from the ground as he devoured her with a kiss.

Kate watched the scene—the tall, powerful man, dressed in his customary jeans and T-shirt and the slender, immaculately groomed girl who was laughing and smiling in his arms. The two of them were so beautiful in their opposite ways. They would indeed make a supremely striking couple.

The thought drove through her like a knife-thrust. Hurriedly, Kate glanced away.

She could sense more than see the chattering group as Giles now was dutifully introduced. Kate closed her eyes and put up a prayer. 'Please don't let him introduce her to me!'

He did not. He did not need to—for a moment later Kate turned in response to a tap on the window and a mimed request for her to wind it down. Feeling her heart freeze within her, wordlessly, she obeyed.

If such a thing were humanly possible, Carmen was even more beautiful close to.

She leaned towards Kate in a cloud of French scent and smiled at her with warm brown eyes. 'Hi, I'm Carmen,' she offered brightly, extending one immaculately manicured hand. 'I want to invite you to join us for dinner tonight.' Her glossy lips parted in a smile, revealing perfect pearl-white teeth. 'Giles has already accepted, so you mustn't say no. It'll be fun, just the four of us—and I think you deserve an end-of-expedition celebration!'

Of course, there was no way Kate could accept. Such an evening would be about as much fun as being thrown to the lions. But even as Kate struggled to politely excuse herself, Vittorio had approached the car and Carmen was telling him, 'Kate says she'll come. I'll book the table.' Then with a final kiss, as Vittorio climbed back into the car, she leaned towards Kate and waved farewell. 'Till this evening, then. I look forward to seeing you. You can tell me all about Cabayan!'

The drive along seething Roxas Boulevard was conducted in stiff and total silence. 'I'll pick you up at eight,' was Vittorio's only comment, as he dropped her off at her own hotel.

Then he was turning back quickly into the traffic, leaving Kate in a state of nameless dark dread at the prospect of what she was totally certain would prove to be the greatest ordeal of her entire life.

CHAPTER EIGHT

At least now there need be no more heart-searching. Kate's decision had been made, finally and irrevocably, the moment she had looked into Carmen's eyes.

She could not have an affair with Vittorio. It simply could not be.

As long as Carmen had been no more than a name and an idea, just possibly, she might have succumbed. To be honest, 'just possibly' was not entirely accurate. For she had more or less decided that she would.

Now she knew that decision had been wrong. Wrong for a dozen different reasons.

Carmen, she now realised, did not deserve her treachery, and she herself deserved better too. To be the short-lived plaything of some arrogant man, to be enjoyed, then discarded like some cheap plastic toy, was not a fate she ought ever to have seriously considered.

OK, so she would have nothing to remember— but at least she would have nothing to regret.

Head high, she regarded her reflection in the mirror, grateful that she had come to her senses at last. She must face the truth and face it with dignity. She loved Vittorio, but he would never be hers. To have had him on those terms, briefly, illicitly, would only have injured her self-respect.

She turned away wearily. Alas, self-respect was no balm for an aching heart. And right now her heart was throbbing with misery to know the path that she must take.

First, she must somehow endure this evening, and then, without telling him, she must immediately leave and head back to London on the first flight available. It would mean breaking her promise to him, but it had been a worthless promise anyway. He'd had no right in the first place to demand it.

She glanced at her watch. There were seven whole hours before he was due to pick her up. She crossed to the bed and sank gratefully on to it—it seemed like ages since she had known the luxury of a proper bed!—then she dropped against the pillows and closed her eyes.

Sleep. That for the moment was all she craved.

It was growing dark when she awoke and she had to switch on the table lamp to see the time. The hands of her watch showed just after seven. She had slept, deliciously, for over six hours. And now she had three-quarters of an hour to get prepared.

Kate showered quickly and dried her hair, then crossed to the wardrobe and pulled the doors open, feeling a smile touch her lips at the row of clothes that hung there. After nothing but the same old trousers and shirt for virtually the entire time she had spent in the jungle, suddenly she felt quite spoilt for choice. It would be a positive luxury to wear a dress again!

She chose a simple blue dress with a wide scoop neckline and brushed her hair back from her face. Then she slipped her feet into high-heeled sandals and gave her reflection a critical glance.

What she saw both pleased her and surprised her a little. For she looked frighteningly composed, as though the decision she had taken, after all the tortured hours of agonising, had miraculously restored her equilibrium.

In her heart she might be feeling as hopeless as a condemned man on his way to his execution, but at least she was making her way there with her head held high. Nobody, she vowed grimly, and least of all Vittorio, would be permitted even a glimpse of her private agony. Her fierce Irish pride would never allow it!

At that moment the phone beside the bed began to ring. Her hand impressively steady, Kate reached to pick it up.

It was the hotel receptionist. He told her, 'Mr de Esquerez is waiting for you downstairs.'

Kate took a deep breath. 'I'll be down in a minute.' Then, closing her eyes, she laid down the phone and put up a silent, heartfelt prayer. Please, lord, she entreated, just give me the strength to get through this evening without falling apart.

But as she stepped out of the lift and saw him standing in the lobby her composure nearly shattered at her feet. Just the sight of him tore her soul to tiny pieces.

Kate had forgotten how magnificent he looked in a suit. Over the past days she had grown so accustomed to his faded jeans and equally faded T-shirts, to a casual, somehow rougher image, that the sight of his tall figure in an immaculate dark suit, the raven-black hair brushed back glossily from his face, almost caused her to cry out loud with pain.

He looked so astounding, so breathtakingly handsome, and every proud inch the worthy descendant of his aristocratic Spanish forebears.

He came towards her with a smile on his lips, yet, she thought, with just a slight air of hesitation.

Her heart squeezed painfully within her. He had no right to torment her like this.

'You're looking lovely.' His greeting was pure charm. But then, of course, he had never lacked charm. And perhaps he was still hoping, Kate thought cynically, that she might agree to be his lover for a while.

Kate fought back the warmth that flooded her loins at that thought and forced herself to meet his eyes boldly. 'You're looking considerably more civilised yourself!'

Vittorio smiled—that easy smile of his that could light up her soul and melt her innards. 'Come. The car's waiting.' He touched her arm. Then he was leading her on brisk strides across the lobby.

It was not the Nissan to which he led her, down the hotel steps and across the forecourt, but a long, low limousine, a Cadillac, all gleaming black paintwork and silvery chrome.

Kate sank into the passenger seat, feeling the strangeness of the car somehow intensify the discomfort of her situation. Was the car his or was it Carmen's? she found herself wondering, as he climbed in beside her. There were so many small facets of his life that were, and would remain always, unknown to her.

She kept her eyes carefully averted as he switched on the engine and adjusted the air-conditioning. 'Is that cool enough for you?' he asked her, as delicious cool air wafted over her.

She nodded. 'It's perfect.' But all she could think of, as the car moved soundlessly forward into the hectic night-time traffic of Roxas Boulevard, was how she was going to get through the evening.

How could she bear to sit there at some dinner table with him and Carmen there together? How could she endure to watch their smiles and glances, their exchange of kisses, touches, caresses?

She closed her eyes and strove to breathe slowly to control the sudden pounding within her. It would have been better if she had refused the invitation, pleaded a headache or total exhaustion, anything rather than actually go through with it. She licked dry lips as a wild thought occurred to her. Perhaps there was still time to chicken out. If she were to plead that she had suddenly been overcome by faintness and ask him to take her back to her hotel, he would, most probably, be delighted to oblige. After all, it was unlikely that he wanted this cosy little foursome any more than she did herself.

She clenched her fists. Yes, she would do it! It was the only exit available to her now. She took a deep breath and half turned towards him. 'Vittorio, I——' she began. But then she blinked in confusion as she glanced through the windscreen. This wasn't Roxas Boulevard they were on any more!

Instantly forgetting what she had been planning to say, she demanded instead, 'Where are you taking me?'

His gaze did not flicker from the road. 'I'm taking you somewhere where we can be alone.'

Kate understood instantly. To some sleazy hotel, where he could make hurried love to her, that, no doubt, was where he was taking her! In his arrogance he had assumed he had her compliance. He had not bothered to wait for her answer.

She rounded on him furiously. 'Take me back to the hotel! I'm not going anywhere with you!'

'Oh, yes, you are. There's no way of getting out of it. Unless, of course, you plan to throw yourself from the car.'

Even Kate had to confess that would be a little extreme. As a mere ploy to stop him having his way, suicide would be a slightly over-the-top gesture. She glared across at him. 'The others will be waiting. I don't know how you expect to get away with this.'

'No one will be waiting. The dinner has been cancelled. Giles decided he was too tired.'

As he glanced across at her, as they turned down a side street, just for a moment, Kate thought she detected a strange look in his eyes. A shadowy flicker of uneasiness that she had never seen before.

Then he added peremptorily, in a tone that was more familiar. 'I'm afraid, *querida*, it's just me and you.'

That was what he thought, but he was mistaken! He had evidently cold-bloodedly engineered this whole thing, but he was in for a nasty surprise. As soon as they had got where they were going to, she would catch the first taxi back to her hotel!

But then, all at once, they had come to a halt and he was leaning across to open up her door for her. And as Kate glanced round her she could see that they were parked, not, as she had fully expected, outside some sleazy backstreet hotel, but in front of the elegant façade of what looked like an exclusive and expensive restaurant.

She blinked back at Vittorio. 'This is a restaurant!'

'Of course it's a restaurant. I'm taking you to dinner.' Then as she frowned, perplexed, he reached for her hand. 'Don't worry, *querida*. I shall explain everything.'

Outrage, in an instant, had mellowed to curiosity. Without another word Kate climbed from the car and followed closely at Vittorio's heels as they were ushered into the restaurant's lavish interior.

The *maître d'* was obviously familiar with Vittorio. He led them across the claret-coloured carpet to a discreet and candle-lit table for two, laid with fine white linen and twinkling silver, and handed each of them a menu. 'Would you like to order an aperitif?'

Kate shook her head, impatient with the delays, as Vittorio ordered himself a whisky. Was he playing some kind of game with her? she found herself wondering with flickering indignation. Although, in truth, all at once, she severely doubted that. The uneasiness she had sensed in him before was even more apparent now.

'Well?' As the cat-footed *maître d'* padded off, Kate leaned across the table towards Vittorio. 'Perhaps you wouldn't mind telling me what this is all about?'

'I'm about to, *querida*.' He leaned back in his seat, the dark-tanned face composed and expressionless. Then he paused for a moment. 'Where shall I start?' Then he immediately proceeded to answer his own question. 'I think, in this particular instance, it would make things easier if I started at the end.'

He paused again and licked his lips and folded his arms across his chest. 'There's been a slight alteration in my personal circumstances since the last time you and I saw each other.' Another slight hesitation, then he told her, 'Carmen and I have finally split up.'

As the calm announcement burst like a landmine between them, Kate could feel the ebony-black eyes scrutinising her face for some reaction. And though she could feel the blood rush through her veins—astonishment? disbelief? relief? incredulity?—she was at great pains to keep her emotions hidden. Her only response was a monosyllabic, 'Why?'

At that moment the waiter appeared with Vittorio's whisky. He took it and informed him, 'We'll order in a moment.' Then, as the waiter departed, he returned to Kate's question. 'In order to explain why I must start at the beginning.'

He raised the whisky to his lips and drank back a mouthful, then laid the glass down again. The black brows frowned. He leaned forward a little—and Kate's heart was jumping like a frog in her chest. Why was he telling her this? She hardly dared wonder. Perhaps all he was after was a sympathetic ear.

'Carmen and I have known one another since childhood,' he began. 'Our families are exceedingly close. It has more or less always just been assumed that one day we would marry.'

His words came back to her, 'We are expected to marry.' Kate's fingers twisted nervously beneath the tablecloth.

'However, in spite of that,' he continued, 'although we both believed that we would marry one day, too, we never got round to an official engagement, let alone to making plans for a wedding. She was busy, studying at first, then later on building up her career. I was always about to set off on yet another expedition. Then, all of a sudden, ten years had passed and we were turning into a pair of permanent "almost fiancés"

'Of course, people were talking, especially our families who never gave up urging us to make a move—but, somehow, we always had our excuses to postpone it just a while longer, though we never bothered to ask each other why.

'And then——' He shook his head and looked down at his hands. 'And then Carmen met another man. He's a Hong Kong banker, a very rich man, and he was desperate to marry Carmen.'

At the flat note in his voice, Kate felt her fears confirmed, and beneath the tablecloth her fingers twisted even more furiously. It was nothing but her sympathy he was after.

Raising his eyes, Vittorio continued, 'Carmen told me all about it just a couple of months ago. And, though I confess, at first, I was slightly shattered, for the first time in our relationship we had a serious talk.' He smiled a little and shook his head. 'It's amazing how self-deceiving we humans can be. Once we'd looked the problem in the face we both realised *why* we'd never got engaged. All the excuses we'd been making for all these years camouflaged a very simple truth. Neither of us really *wanted* to get married. We knew we were totally wrong for one another.'

Kate blinked at him. Her fingers grew still. 'Wrong?' she repeated. 'Wrong in what way?'

'In every way, *querida*.' His expression softened. 'Can you imagine Carmen trekking through the jungle or sleeping in a tent the way you did?' He rejected with a smile the very notion. 'Just discovering a run in her tights is almost enough to give her a nervous breakdown! She's far more interested, and always has been, in the cut of my jackets than in the work I'm doing.'

His expression sobered as he paused for a moment. 'Don't think for a moment that I'm running her down. She's put up with my gallivanting through the jungle and turning up on her doorstep in grubby T-shirt and jeans without ever making a single complaint. She's never tried to change me, I'll grant her that. But all the same, as we both finally realised, there are far too many differences between us for a marriage ever to work. We love each other, and we probably always will, but it's the love, not of lovers, but rather of friends.'

Kate was sitting very still, her ankles twined together so ferociously tightly the bones seemed in imminent danger of cracking. All the things he was saying were indisputable. She had observed many of them for herself. 'So, why didn't you break off your relationship immediately? Why did you wait till now to do it?'

Vittorio leaned back again in his chair. 'One thing Carmen and I do most definitely have in common is a respect for tradition, and respect for our families. We owed it to them to be very certain before we made such a drastic decision. So we agreed that we would use my next expedition as a time for us each to consider our position. Away from one another we'd have a chance to think and hopefully see the situation more clearly.'

He smiled a disarmingly lopsided smile. 'Of course I didn't realise that you'd be tagging along and giving me very little chance to think!'

Kate felt herself flush a deep shade of pink. 'No wonder you were so delighted to see me! If I'd known you were in the midst of a personal crisis, I promise you, I would have kept my distance.'

'I'm glad you didn't.' He leaned towards her. 'Seeing the way you coped with things made me realise, perhaps for the first time in my life, that the type of girl I need, a girl like you, really does exist, after all. I was so used to Carmen I'd begun to think that the entire female race was a copy of her—in which case, there wasn't a great deal of point in my bothering to look for someone different.'

The type of girl I need, a girl like you . . . 'A girl like you', not just a simple 'you'. There was a world of difference between the two. Kate tried to keep the disappointment from her voice. 'Well, I'm glad I helped to make up your mind for you.'

'I think my mind was already made up.' Vittorio smiled and leaned across the table to touch her arm softly. 'But you definitely helped me to realise that the decision I'd made was the right one.' He paused, letting his eyes drift over her face, their expression intense, their blackness penetrating. 'I would have told you the truth, for you must have wondered what the devil was going on. One minute I was seducing you, the next retreating. I was acting like a crazy man.

'I wanted to tell you.' His tone was earnest. 'I wanted to tell you more than you can know.' He broke off abruptly. 'But there was one other problem. Carmen and I had promised each other that if one of us decided that we should go ahead and get married anyway, the other would, without question, accept that decision. That was another reason I didn't tell you. I still didn't know how things would turn out.'

He frowned at the confusion on her face and reached down to retrieve one nervously twisting hand. 'You see, I had to speak to Carmen first. That was why I asked you not to leave the Philippines without telling me. However things turned out, I owed you an explanation.'

So, she had been wrong yet again. It had not been an affair he had been proposing. He had simply wanted a chance to explain.

Kate stared at him wordlessly as he went on to tell her, 'It was only after Carmen and I had a long chat this afternoon that I knew for certain I was free. She's decided to go ahead and marry her Hong Kong banker.'

But why was he telling her all this? Why was he talking about being free? And why was he holding her hand so tightly, as though he would never let her go?

'What would have happened,' he was asking now, 'if I had in fact told you all this earlier? Would it have made any difference to you?'

'I don't know.' How could she answer? What sort of difference did he mean?

He sighed and let his eyes drop down again. 'I know it would have made a difference to me if the relationship had been ended before I met you.'

Kate stared at his lowered lashes and the cleft in his chin. She scarcely dared to listen to what he might say next.

'If there had been no Carmen to consider...' his eyes swept upwards, making her heart stop '...I would have been free to tell you that I love you.'

'Love?' She swallowed. 'Love?' she said again.

He nodded. 'Love. *Si, amor.*' He held her hand more tightly, black eyes burning like coals. 'If I had told you that, what would you have told me?'

A weak foolish smile crept round Kate's lips. 'Why, that I love you, too,' she answered simply.

He was almost as disbelieving as she. 'Do you mean that, *querida?*' he wanted to know.

She laughed. 'Vittorio Felipe Salvador de Esquerez, how dare you question my Irish integrity?'

Then he was leaning across the table to kiss her. '*Querida, querida,* my dreams have come true!'

Next instant he was simultaneously beckoning to the waiter, flinging a wad of notes down on the table, and grabbing Kate firmly by the arm to hustle her out to the waiting car.

'Where are we going?' she demanded, laughing, loving the sheer, wild impetuosity of him. 'We haven't eaten yet!'

'We'll eat later,' he assured her, gunning the engine. He kissed her again and squeezed her close to him. 'But right now I want to be alone with you.'

It was less than ten dizzy minutes later that they were stepping into the lift at the Manila Hotel and heading for his suite on the third floor. And his arms were about her, almost carrying her bodily, as he swept her along the silent corridor.

Then at last, at last, the suite door clicked behind them, and for a moment the two of them just stood there silently, each as overcome with emotion as the other, as they gazed helplessly into one another's eyes. Then Vittorio reached out to touch her hair, sending shivers of sensation right down to Kate's toes, and, as naturally as breathing, she leaned against him and slid her arms around his neck.

He pulled her even closer, strong arms encircling her, and nuzzled his face against her hair. 'If you knew how desperately I've waited for this moment.'

His voice was harsh with the wanting that throbbed in him, as he kissed her earlobe, her chin, her face. 'But I dared not love you in case I might lose you. It would not have been fair to you, nor to myself.'

Kate could not have spoken if her life had depended on it. The emotions, the sensations that were rocketing through her, had snatched away her power of speech.

She sighed as his hands caressed her shoulders, the small of her back, the soft skin of her neck. To think that all the time she had been longing for him so desperately he, equally desperately, had been longing for her! It made her weak with happiness to know the truth at last and to feel bound to him by this need so long denied.

His lips were on her lips, crushing her, burning her, sending her senses up in flames. Then his hand was moving round to caress her breasts, making her sigh and sink against him, weakly, wanting him.

'There's just one thing,' he murmured against her cheekbone as, without a word spoken, they were heading towards the bedroom. 'Just one question you must answer. Something I have to know.'

She raised her flushed face to look into his eyes. 'I'll tell you anything. Anything at all.'

He smiled. '*Querida*, just tell me that you love me—and that you will do me the honour of becoming my wife.'

The endless blackness of his eyes burned into her.

He was waiting.

She answered with a simple, 'Yes.'

Then they were stumbling—laughing, weeping, hugging—through the open door into the bedroom beyond. And everything that either of them had ever longed for, they knew in their hearts, was with them now.

The sun was shining when they stepped off the plane at Dublin's Shannon Airport, the tall, dark man in the navy blue suit and the green-eyed, golden-haired girl at his side.

'So, this is Ireland.' Vittorio took Kate's arm. 'It looks almost as beautiful as you, *querida*.'

Flushed with excitement, Kate turned to look up at him. 'Oh, it's far more beautiful than I am,' she promised. 'And over the next two weeks I plan to show you every precious inch of it.'

Vittorio laughed and hugged her to him. *'Mi amor,'* he murmured. 'How much I love you.'

He had told her that often over the past few weeks and she knew she would never tire of hearing it—just as she would never tire of the sight of his face, the sound of his voice or the touch of his hand. He was her everything. He always would be.

Their last few days together in the Philippines had been hectic. There had been the future to plan and the past to explain. And this time the explanations were Kate's.

Over breakfast on their first morning back from Cabayan, after an unforgettable night of love, Vittorio had demanded, 'Now it's your turn to come clean. I want to know exactly why this story meant so much to you—why you were prepared virtually to risk your life to get it.'

They were seated at the breakfast table in Vittorio's suite bedroom, he dressed only in pyjama bottoms, she in the missing pyjama top. Kate crunched on her toast. 'I already told you. I was in danger of losing my job if I didn't.'

He sat back in his chair. 'Why?' he asked.

'It's a long, boring story.' Kate made a face. 'But the short version is that the company that owns *Deadline* lost a lot of money on another venture and had to make certain cost-saving cuts. Specifically that meant making do with just one foreign affairs reporter instead of the previous two. Either me or my colleague, Roy, had to go.'

'You mean they were just going to throw you out, just like that?'

Kate shook her head. 'No, they wouldn't do that. They're a decent company. They treat their staff well. What they were going to do was demote one of us to home affairs reporter—though even that isn't quite as bad as it sounds. It would have meant a cut in pay for one of us, but the loser would still have been earning more than most journalists on similar magazines.'

Vittorio was watching her. He cut in suddenly. 'But you couldn't afford a pay cut, could you? Or, rather, your family couldn't afford for you to take a pay cut.'

Kate blinked at him. Was he some kind of mind reader? 'How did you know that?' she queried.

'Because I know you, *mi dulce amor*.' He reached across the table for her hand. 'Your father is jobless, you have six brothers and sisters and you're the eldest. In your eyes that makes you responsible,' he told her softly.

'I had to help them.' She was almost defensive. She'd had no idea he understood her so well.

Still holding her hand, Vittorio moved his chair round beside her. Watching her through his lashes, he bent to kiss her hand. 'Now tell me where your brother fits into all of this. That's the only thing I haven't quite figured out.'

'You mean Liam?'

'I mean the one who's studying to be a doctor.'

Kate nodded. 'That's Liam.' She sighed. 'It's very simple. If I was earning less money, I'd never be able to manage the mortgage repayments on my flat. There's no way I could cut down the money I send my parents. They need every single penny of it. So, I would have to sell up and Liam would never hear of it. He would do something crazy like give up his studies and take a job as a pharmacist or something, so he could contribute to our parents, too, and allow me to cut down my contribution a bit.'

'And you didn't want Liam to give up his studies?'

'Absolutely not!' Kate was vehement. 'I had a hard enough job persuading him in the first place that he ought to go ahead and become a doctor. The crazy fool was all for wasting his talents—he'll make the best doctor that ever lived, I promise you—and going out to find a job as soon as he left school.'

'Isn't that what you did?'

The question surprised her. 'Yes, but that was different,' she defended. 'I was the eldest. There was no one else to help.'

'Oh, *querida, querida*...' He was reaching out for her, drawing her softly into his arms. 'How much I love you. How very much I love you. You are the most wonderful young woman in all the world.' He hugged her and kissed her and pushed back her hair and looked long and lovingly into her eyes.

'So, this job of yours.' He smiled at her softly. 'This contest between you and your colleague, Roy, for the one remaining job of foreign affairs reporter... Was it to be a case of the best man wins?'

Kate nodded, loving him, overwhelmed by his love for her. 'The editor decided that, over a period of six months, the reporter who turned in the most valuable stories—in other words, the most stories to make the front cover—would be the one to stay on the foreign news desk.' She sighed. 'Over the past four months Roy came up with two real corkers, whereas I didn't come up with a single thing.' She omitted the sad story of the Hong Kong fiasco and ended, 'Cabayan was my last chance.'

'Now I understand.' Vittorio was smiling. 'Thank heavens for Roy—and Cabayan!'

Amen to that! As his arms had folded around her, Kate had suddenly realised that what, at the time, had felt like such a disastrous run of bad luck, when all those front cover stories were so cruelly eluding her, had in fact been the luckiest break of her life! Had she not been so desperate to get the Cabayan story, she and Vittorio would never have met!

After the explanations had come the introductions to Vittorio's family. The uncles, the cousins, the sisters, the brothers—in addition, of course, to his wonderful parents, who, like all the others of the vast Esquerez clan, had welcomed Kate with open arms.

And the warm welcome had partly been thanks to Carmen. For Vittorio's charming dark-haired ex-girlfriend had been at pains to adopt the newcomer as a friend, singing her praises to Vittorio's family and announcing to the world how happy she was that Vittorio had found the right girl at last.

'He'll make you happy,' she had confided to Kate, 'and I can see for myself that you make him happier than he has ever been before.' Then she'd kissed her new friend and embraced her. 'Take good care of him. He's a very special man.'

Kate had smiled back at her, touched and grateful. 'We'll never forget your kindness, you know.'

The dark-haired girl had shrugged off the compliment. 'Just think of each other—and have a wonderful life together.'

That they would was something Kate had no doubts about. As she had sat in the breathtakingly palatial surroundings of his parents' home up north in Baguio, listening to the excited and lavish arrangements that were being made for their wedding in just two months' time, Kate had occasionally found her thoughts drifting to the day when their real life together would begin.

They had agreed that they would work together on the Esquerez special village projects, Vittorio, as always, handling the general administration, with Kate in charge of the more day-to-day problems. She would make herself an expert, she had vowed to Vittorio. She even had plans to write a book.

He had kissed her proudly and rumpled her hair. 'I think I should make you our publicist, too. You can be in charge of ensuring that all the information that reaches the public is true. That will put a stop to any future Ramoses.'

Kate had smiled at the significance of that remark. Ramos himself would bother them no more. Currently in police custody on various charges of fraud, he seemed set for a lengthy custodial sentence. And his involvement in the Cabayan project had already been terminated. Vittorio had reimbursed the money that Ramos had paid the expedition, and then taken the grateful professor under the Esquerez wing. The future of the tribe was now assured.

'Of course I'll be your publicist,' she'd agreed. 'And the first thing I intend to do is improve your standing with the Press. I want them and the rest of the world to know what a wonderful man you really are.'

He'd kissed her nose. 'If you insist. But the only one I want to think I'm wonderful is you.'

Kate had written her article on the Cabayan tribe on her lone homeward flight from Manila to London, and presented it, along with her notice, to *Deadline*'s editor just two days later.

Derek had been delighted with the former— 'You've done a first-class job. This is a must for the front cover!'—but he had been openly regretful about her resignation. 'The magazine will miss you,' he'd told her sincerely. 'You've made a significant contribution over the years.'

Still it had left the way open for her colleague, Roy, to pick up the lone mantle of foreign affairs reporter, and Kate had felt genuinely pleased for him. She had felt even more pleased when Derek had gone out of his way to speed up her departure from the company. 'I know you're just dying to get back with that man of yours. I can see it in every lovesick line of your face!'

He'd been absolutely right. In spite of Vittorio's daily phone calls, being physically apart from him was like a constant pain. Climbing on to the plane at Manila airport to make the flight back to London alone had been the hardest thing Kate had ever had to do. But in the end, the separation had been tolerably brief. By the time her various bits of leave were added together Derek had insisted only on her serving out a couple of weeks.

Then, not a moment too soon, Vittorio had flown in from Manila to help her organise the shipping of her belongings to the Philippines—and, of course, to meet her beloved Liam, before accompanying her to Ireland to meet the rest of her family.

Liam had fallen instantly under his spell. 'He's the man for you,' he had told Kate, hugging her. 'I couldn't have done better if I'd picked him for you myself!'

There had been only one brief moment of friction between the two future brothers-in-law, and that had been when Vittorio had insisted that he should assume the financial burden of assisting Liam's and Kate's parents.

'Just you concentrate on becoming a doctor,' he had insisted, echoing Kate's own oft-repeated words. 'Then you can help them all you want to.'

And in the end, reluctantly, Liam had agreed. 'One day, I'll pay you both back,' he had promised.

As they headed now through the bustling halls of Shannon Airport, Kate's heart was thumping with excitement. 'I hope you're ready for the onslaught,' she joked to Vittorio, squeezing his arm. 'My family are a pretty exuberant lot, and I've a suspicion there's quite a crowd of them waiting outside.'

Vittorio grinned down at her, black-eyed and handsome, making her heart squeeze with helpless joy in her chest. 'I can't wait to meet them,' he assured her. 'They're my family too now, after all.'

As he bent to brush her hair with his lips, Kate felt the love and the happiness within her rise up in a fierce, unstoppable tide. Her mouth puckered with emotion. She blinked back the tears.

'I love you, Vittorio,' she breathed.

'I love you, too, *querida*. With all my heart.'

Then they were striding out towards the exit, their future, their past, their present all around them, now and for ever, side by side.

OVER THE YEARS, TELEVISION HAS BROUGHT
THE LIVES AND LOVES OF MANY CHARACTERS INTO
YOUR HOMES. NOW HARLEQUIN INTRODUCES YOU
TO THE TOWN AND PEOPLE OF

One small town—twelve terrific love stories.

GREAT READING...GREAT SAVINGS...AND A FABULOUS
FREE GIFT!

Each book set in Tyler is a self-contained love story; together, the
twelve novels stitch the fabric of the community.

By collecting proofs-of-purchase found in each Tyler book, you can
receive a fabulous gift, ABSOLUTELY FREE! And use our special
Tyler coupons to save on your next TYLER book purchase.

Join us for the fourth TYLER book,
MONKEY WRENCH by Nancy Martin.

*Can elderly Rose Atkins successfully bring a new love into
granddaughter Susannah's life?*

If you missed *Whirlwind* (March), *Bright Hopes* (April) or *Wisconsin Wedding* (May), and would
like to order them, send your name, address, zip or postal code, along with a check or money
order for $3.99 (please do not send cash), plus 75¢ postage and handling ($1.00 in Canada),
for each book ordered, payable to Harlequin Reader Service to:

In the U.S.
3010 Walden Avenue
P.O. Box 1325
Buffalo, NY 14269-1325

In Canada
P.O. Box 609
Fort Erie, Ontario
L2A 5X3

Please specify book title(s) with your order.
Canadian residents add applicable federal and provincial taxes.

TYLER-4

"GET AWAY FROM IT ALL" SWEEPSTAKES

HERE'S HOW THE SWEEPSTAKES WORKS

NO PURCHASE NECESSARY

To enter each drawing, complete the appropriate Official Entry Form or a 3" by 5" index card by hand-printing your name, address and phone number and the trip destination that the entry is being submitted for (i.e., Caneel Bay, Canyon Ranch or London and the English Countryside) and mailing it to: Get Away From It All Sweepstakes, P.O. Box 1397, Buffalo, New York 14269-1397.

No responsibility is assumed for lost, late or misdirected mail. Entries must be sent separately with first class postage affixed, and be received by: 4/15/92 for the Caneel Bay Vacation Drawing, 5/15/92 for the Canyon Ranch Vacation Drawing and 6/15/92 for the London and the English Countryside Vacation Drawing. Sweepstakes is open to residents of the U.S. (except Puerto Rico) and Canada, 21 years of age or older as of 5/31/92.

For complete rules send a self-addressed, stamped (WA residents need not affix return postage) envelope to: Get Away From It All Sweepstakes, P.O. Box 4892, Blair, NE 68009.

© 1992 HARLEQUIN ENTERPRISES LTD.   SWP-RLS

- -

"GET AWAY FROM IT ALL" SWEEPSTAKES

HERE'S HOW THE SWEEPSTAKES WORKS

NO PURCHASE NECESSARY

To enter each drawing, complete the appropriate Official Entry Form or a 3" by 5" index card by hand-printing your name, address and phone number and the trip destination that the entry is being submitted for (i.e., Caneel Bay, Canyon Ranch or London and the English Countryside) and mailing it to: Get Away From It All Sweepstakes, P.O. Box 1397, Buffalo, New York 14269-1397.

No responsibility is assumed for lost, late or misdirected mail. Entries must be sent separately with first class postage affixed, and be received by: 4/15/92 for the Caneel Bay Vacation Drawing; 5/15/92 for the Canyon Ranch Vacation Drawing and 6/15/92 for the London and the English Countryside Vacation Drawing. Sweepstakes is open to residents of the U.S. (except Puerto Rico) and Canada, 21 years of age or older as of 5/31/92.

For complete rules send a self-addressed, stamped (WA residents need not affix return postage) envelope to: Get Away From It All Sweepstakes, P.O. Box 4892, Blair, NE 68009.

© 1992 HARLEQUIN ENTERPRISES LTD.   SWP-RLS

"GET AWAY FROM IT ALL"

Brand-new Subscribers-Only Sweepstakes
OFFICIAL ENTRY FORM

This entry must be received by: April 15, 1992
This month's winner will be notified by: April 30, 1992
Trip must be taken between: May 31, 1992—May 31, 1993

YES, I want to win the Caneel Bay Plantation vacation for
two. I understand the prize includes round-trip airfare and the
two additional prizes revealed in the BONUS PRIZES insert.

Name _____

Address _____

City _____

State/Prov._____ Zip/Postal Code _____

Daytime phone number _____
                                            (Area Code)

Return entries with invoice in envelope provided. Each book in this shipment has two
entry coupons — and the more coupons you enter, the better your chances of winning!
© 1992 HARLEQUIN ENTERPRISES LTD.   1M-CPN

"GET AWAY FROM IT ALL"

Brand-new Subscribers-Only Sweepstakes
OFFICIAL ENTRY FORM

This entry must be received by: April 15, 1992
This month's winner will be notified by: April 30, 1992
Trip must be taken between: May 31, 1992—May 31, 1993

YES, I want to win the Caneel Bay Plantation vacation for
two. I understand the prize includes round-trip airfare and the
two additional prizes revealed in the BONUS PRIZES insert.

Name _____

Address _____

City _____

State/Prov._____ Zip/Postal Code _____

Daytime phone number _____
                                            (Area Code)

Return entries with invoice in envelope provided. Each book in this shipment has two
entry coupons — and the more coupons you enter, the better your chances of winning!
© 1992 HARLEQUIN ENTERPRISES LTD.   1M-CPN